Where The
RAINBOW
Ends

Also by Anurag Anand

The Legend of Amrapali

Of Tattoos and Taboos!

Reality ~~Bytes~~ Bites.

The Quest for Nothing!

Where The
RAINBOW
Ends

Anurag Anand

Srishti
PUBLISHERS & DISTRIBUTORS

SRISHTI PUBLISHERS & DISTRIBUTORS
N-16, C. R. Park
New Delhi 110 019
editorial@srishtipublishers.com

First published by
Srishti Publishers & Distributors in 2013

Typeset by Eshu Graphic

For Naisha,
my little bundle of immeasurable joy

One

Obviously the economic pundits and politicos, who can't seem to stop raving about Human Capital, deemed to serve as a catapult for propelling India into the coveted league of developed nations, have missed out on a crucial point somewhere. Or perhaps the perks accompanying their V.I.P. statuses have so distanced them from reality that they are able to see an illusionary promise even in the sea of utterly hopeless humanity that surrounds us morning through night.

As far as I go, there isn't a tinge of optimism I can feel about the sweaty, stinking oaf - a quintal-plus would be my most conservative estimate of his weight – ahead of me, who has been spraying my crotch with poisonous, ill-smelling vapours ever since I joined the queue. Well, perhaps I am being a tad harsh on the fellow who has visibly been betrayed by his own digestive juices, a victim himself, and is clearly in the need for some sympathy and a very strong antacid. But what about the lady there, dragging two defiant and wailing brats as if they were items she had forgotten to check-in? Or that man screaming his guts out into the phone, leaving me in little doubt that the fellow on the other end was either deaf or marooned on an island where the telecom companies were yet to erect towers? If this is the bunch we think will steer us to our promised glories, well, God save Mother India.

Anyway, after being adequately frisked and felt by a perverse-looking member of the airport security staff I was eased into another crammed-to-the-hilt zone - the departure lounge. I glanced at my watch, an Espirit timepiece I had received as a gift on my last birthday. Forty minutes, I still had forty long minutes to kill before boarding. Hopefully!

I glanced around for an empty seat (realising delightfully that my supply of optimism hadn't entirely waned) and not finding even a single one, settled for leaning against a vending machine to unfold the newspaper I had been clutching. I had plenty of things playing on my mind and knowing myself for as long as I had, 34 years to be precise, I couldn't allow my thoughts to run amok and distract me from my immediate objective of boarding the plane.

In contradiction to the horrific tales of delayed departures I had heard, the boarding was announced on time and we were herded inside the craft. I had been allotted an aisle seat. And thankfully the man preceding me in the check-in queue was now separated from me by at least five rows of well-padded seats. Some benevolent soul had saved my nasal glands from certain torture and potential impairment, and I could only close my eyes in a silent expression of gratitude.

The cabin crew comprised all of three people - a young man and two women, all in their early twenties or thereabouts. It was a budget carrier after all, and for the sake of sound commerce they had to make do with the minimum possible headcount. I can appreciate the perspective of the airline management, but the three poor souls designed to bear the strategy's brunt were having somewhat harrowing a time.

Stuffing ill-sized baggage into overhead compartments while passengers waited on them with an aura of aristocracy, as if the flight ticket entitled them to a brief stint of feudality, and scurrying about to deliver water bottles to impatient travellers, the crew members were getting a taste of reality that doesn't usually find its way into the airline hiring brochures. Cattle class, wasn't that the term an esteemed statesman had bestowed upon this phenomenon? How apt, but only if one ignored the minor subtlety that the remark eventually resulted in his ouster from office (or was it resignation, a more responsible but equally baffling act, considering we are a democracy that guarantees everyone the right of expression).

As the plane began to crawl, crew members took their positions, demonstrating how to efficiently buckle and unbuckle a seat-belt and other such. One of them, whose name I read on her breast-plate, Rochelle, was standing right in front of me and mechanically going about her duties. I glanced at her with comical curiosity, wondering how she endured a task of such insipid nature without as much as a frown on her face, my gaze lingering for just a wee bit longer than intended. A genial smile was affixed on her face-a cultivated facade to conceal her private self from those she met during the course of her work.

She was just like *Her*. Or maybe she wasn't. Who am I trying to fool here? Had it been the other hostess and not Rochelle who was in the periphery of my vision, would I have stopped from drawing parallels then? The answer is no. My mind, and more so my heart, needed an excuse, no matter how feeble, to begin thinking about Avantika, and Rochelle had served precisely that purpose.

Instantly I was drawn to the day I had first met Avantika, a day that could be traced back by eight calendar months, which now seemed like another lifetime altogether. It was another flight, a premium carrier instead of the budget one I was sitting in now.

Back then my life had been racing on a completely different track. I was among the privileged few, financially at least – a bright corporate executive with a promising career ahead of him, a stud among mules, a man who did not have to endure the travails of travelling cattle class. Though the nature of my travel had been personal, my frequent work-related jaunts had left me with enough reward miles to book myself a business class ticket on my preferred airline.

After disembarking from the coach – a business class exclusive, mind you – I had walked to my seat with the usual arrogance and gait of the privileged, acknowledging greetings from the crew members with only a genial nod. I wasn't wearing a jacket, so when one of the stewards rushed to appease me by helping me with my overnighter instead, I gladly allowed him the pleasure, turning to carefully pick a business magazine from the pile ahead.

The plane was airborne soon and I engrossed myself in figuring out the possible good that could emerge from the elitist tea party underway in Davos, Switzerland, under the garb of The World Economic Forum meeting. Then suddenly, without a warning, a splash of cold liquid, followed by something human tearing its way through the magazine to land in my lap, left me startled and drenched.

'Oh shit,' both of us blurted out at the same time. She was a girl, one of the crew members, and though I had missed witnessing the action, I could guess that she had been carrying a glass of water (thankfully it wasn't orange juice or something) and had tripped, only to deposit the glass, its contents and her own self on me.

It was filmy alright, the occurrence, but nothing of the sort that Bollywood love flicks thrive on happened between us. And when our eyes met, while she struggled to detach herself from my lap, instead of the three blinks and a blush one is accustomed to seeing on the big screen, I only saw embarrassment in them. Not to mention the angry fumes gushing out of my own ears. You might not understand the intensity of my anger now, but then, you were not the one feeling the chill and the tickle from a stream of water carving its way down your underpants.

'Sorry… Sir,' she murmured. And even before I could voice my annoyance, she said, 'I will get you some tissues,' and darted out of my sight. In the little time it took me to survey the damage, she was back with the promised tissues, a whole bunch of them. I looked at her face – totally intent on giving her a piece of my mind – and our eyes met once again, her lips curling into a polite smile. No, it wasn't love at first sight, but the smile did dissuade me from my intended course of action.

'It is alright… Avantika,' I said, glancing at her nameplate and averting my gaze almost instantaneously. Undoubtedly the man who had first decided on the site for pinning nameplates was either a moron or a pervert of unmatched proportions. Why else would someone come up with an idea whereby the simple and chaste act of attempting to read a girl's name could leave a well-meaning man misunderstood and, if luck wasn't on his side, thrashed to tatters?

I grabbed the tissues, turning down her offer to help me wipe the residual water off my clothing, and got down to dealing with the task myself.

My apologies, if I have set your expectations soaring unintentionally; but nothing much transpired between us on that flight, nothing of significance at least. Only exchange of casual glances and knowing smiles, as though we were accomplices in some sort of a covert intelligence operation. And of course, the warm farewell she dished out to me as I disembarked from the plane, which I thought was different from the mechanical goodbyes she was doling out to other flyers, did well to make up for the mishap I had been on the receiving end of. Well, I can't rule out the possibility that she was only going about her usual routine and it was me who was being overly perceptive, but then, what the heck.

However, if you thought that Avantika's chapter was closed from my life, you, like I had been then, are highly mistaken. It was a Saturday, three days after my return from Delhi, and Avantika happened to be the last thing on my mind. Truth be told, I had allowed myself a few flattering smiles thinking about Avantika and the connection we had apparently established over a moment of slight misfortune, but that was only during my way back home from the airport. My life, once it reclaimed me, was in a state of adequate turmoil for my mind to push Avantika and her thoughts into one of its remotest recesses.

The day hadn't begun on a particularly pleasant note even though it fell within the eagerly awaited crevice separating two working weeks. Myra, my five-year-old daughter had woken up with slight fever and a headache. Our residential maid, my only support as far as looking after Myra was concerned, was visiting her village and the replacement she had helped arrange had unceremoniously decided to not turn up. Resultantly, a better part of my morning had gone in tending to a very cranky Myra and cussing the entire species of maids under my breath for heartlessly exploiting and ever so frequently holding us to ransom.

It was after I had successfully relegated hundreds of Shanta*bai*s and Kanta*bai*s to the deepest, darkest dungeons of hell that I thought of putting to test Myra's genetic construct. A movie (some random animation flick I had been desperately trying to avoid) and an ice-cream promised, and she began to exhibit instant signs of recovery. She was my daughter indeed, receptive and responsive to the right set of incentives.

Myra loves escalators, like most other children her age. And kids, as you might have noticed, sometimes have the strangest reasons behind their likes and dislikes. It wasn't the convenience of being carried up or down mall floors without moving one's limb that interested her, but a strange game of balance she had come up with, to my utmost detestation of course. She enjoyed running against the steady rhythm of the escalator, using it as a treadmill of sorts, trying to match her speed so the escalator would fail in its assigned task of ferrying her.

That day too she had brightened up at the sight of the escalator and got engaged in her silly game instantly. I did not resist, partly because she hadn't been keeping well and partly since the mall wasn't crowded yet and she was unlikely to stall other visitors with her act. When I was nearing the landing, she was still somewhere down the middle, holding up against the mechanical forces propelling her opponent.

'*Beta*, hurry or we will miss the movie,' I barked.

I had turned to glance at her in a bid to make my words sound more persuasive and that proved my undoing. I crashed into something (someone, to be precise) and went tumbling down the floor. I wasn't alone. I had company even in that moment of extreme embarrassment. There was someone I was entangled with, a human body – evidently the very individual I had crashed into and taken down with me. My landing had been safe, away from the stirring escalator, and once I had ascertained that my hands and feet were all in place, I made an attempt to get up.

Ignoring wicked smiles from other shoppers and the impish chuckle of Myra, who, by now, had terminated her game in favour of the more entertaining spectacle, I got to my feet. And that was when I saw her. Believe it or not, standing in front of me, dishevelled due to the sudden crash and bang, was Avantika, the air hostess who had left me all wet and soaking only a few days back.

'I am sorry…,' she said, and then she saw me. 'You!' she exclaimed as a flicker of recognition emerged in her eyes.

'Hello to you too,' I responded with a smile. She smiled back. And then, abruptly, as if on the same cue, we burst out laughing. It was a coincidence alright, but someone up there surely had a funny bone and had set this act up perfectly.

'Well, now that you have exacted your revenge, will you please stop stalking me?' she said. 'I mean, I thought you had forgiven me for the accident the other day. I never realised it had offended you so much that you would track me down and do this,' she explained, her hand swaying back a little to point at the exact spot we had landed. I laughed once again. 'By the way, I am Avantika.'

'I know. I am Rahul … Rahul Singh,' I replied, extending my

hand for her to shake.

'And I am Myra … Myra Singh,' I heard, as a small hand emerged from under my outstretched one and reached out towards her. 'My daughter,' I added for Avantika's benefit.

'Hi Myra,' she said, bending down to touch her cheeks. 'You know, other than your father and you, there is another person who likes to offer his introductions in a similar fashion. Bond… James Bond. Ever heard of him?

Avantika was wearing a white cotton dress with olive and saffron floral prints. Her shoulder-length hair had been left loose and she looked very different from the time I had last seen her. Somewhat pale and pinched, due to the missing coat of makeup perhaps, but pretty nevertheless. I wondered how I had managed to recognise her despite her drastically altered appearance. Instantly the thought branched away into another. How did she manage to recognise me? We had met just once in the past and not in a setting ideal for people to remember each other. Was there a chance that she had been thinking about me too? I allowed myself an indulgent smile. Maybe she was. Who knows?

We began walking together, all three of us. Myra and Avantika were already chatting as if they were long lost friends meeting each other after ages - a girl-thing of forging instantaneous bonds that I wasn't, by the sheer virtue of my gender, programmed to comprehend.

'You stay somewhere close by?' I asked her when the first opportunity to talk came my way.

'No, I don't stay here. In fact I don't even stay in Mumbai. I am from Delhi,' she said. 'I was here visiting a colleague for the weekend, but she was summoned to work at the last minute. Some unexpected absenteeism in her team I guess, and since I was left alone, I decided to come here and catch a movie. I am watching….'

'Wow, we are also watching the same movie. We can all see it together,' Myra nearly screamed in excitement. Her invitation for Avantika was more a statement than a request and neither of us had the heart to oppose it.

'I have a compelling reason to endure this crap,' I said to Avantika, looking at Myra from the corner of my eye while waiting for the counter clerk to print the three tickets. 'But why would you deliberately want to subject yourself to an hour and half of torture?'

'All of us have a child within us, don't we? Let's just say that I like listening to that child more than I like listening to the adult me.' Turning to Myra, she added with a wink, 'Plus, not everybody is blessed with a refined taste in entertainment, right?' Next, the two were exchanging high-fives and I could do nothing but watch my own daughter conspire against me with someone she had only just met.

An over-smart canine singing and wooing bitches from the neighbourhood might be somebody's idea of entertainment, but I wasn't impressed. I agree, it was the producer's own money (or of someone he had managed to beguile into investing in the film) that was flowing down the sewers, but I had paid seven hundred and fifty bucks for the tickets and thus had fairly and squarely acquired the rights to voice my dissent.

However, both Myra and Avantika appeared to think otherwise. They were chit-chatting and breaking into abrupt spells of giddy laughter in a manner that could mislead one into believing that the film was worthy of being showcased in an international film festival. Their superlative elation even led me to a moment of self-doubt, but one look at the empty seats around us and the doubt was quickly dispelled.

The movie eventually concluded, a happy ending with the protagonist getting together with the bitch of his choice (like I was expecting anything else to happen), and we headed to a coffee shop. The suggestion had been mine since I desperately needed a shot of caffeine to clear the garbage from my mind. As we took the first sips of our cappuccinos, our eyes met, Avantika's and mine, and I felt a shiver run down my spine. I couldn't tell what it was, but I felt as if she could see right through me – an uneasy feeling, as if she could count the small change in my pockets and read my thoughts too, even as they were being relayed.

But Myra was quick to reclaim her new-found friend by offering her a sip of her milkshake, thereby putting my awkwardness to rest, but not before it had stirred something deep within me. I was suddenly inquisitive. I wanted to talk to Avantika, know more about her, but it was only an exchange of phone numbers I could manage during our first real meeting.

This chance-meeting proved a stepping-stone to a confusing relationship that we embarked upon – Avantika, Myra and me. Every time she was in Mumbai, a frequent occurrence owing to her profession, Avantika would call and visit us. She would spend hours in the company of Myra, playing with her, reading to her and listening to her stories from school with an interest that I had usually struggled to garner. The confusing aspect of our relationship was me.

I could just not figure where I featured in the larger scheme of things. A terrible allegory, but for a better part of the eight months I had known her, I felt like a man intruding between a couple madly in love – a sore thorn of sorts. No, don't get me wrong, Avantika was more than civil towards me. In fact we had settled into a comfort zone, where, when we did manage to steal our moments, I found myself able to discuss anything and everything concerning my life with her. While she remained more of a listener than a talker, empathising or counselling me as per the need of the moment, she had slowly but surely become such an integral part of my life that I couldn't help but wonder if we were just the friends we liked to believe we were.

Avantika had not dropped any perceivable hints and I had

not pressed the issue either for the fear of unsettling the beautiful thing we were already sharing. It was very recently, only a couple of weeks back, that the clouds of uncertainty did clear out on me, on their own, almost accidently. And now, I can't help but blame myself for delaying the inevitable and not seeking out a fix to my dilemma earlier. Perhaps I was too engrossed in weathering the turbulent storms that were persistently attempting to derail my life all this while. To my credit, I had managed to hold on to my life till date, albeit just by the tail, but now that Avantika was gone, I couldn't help but find myself absorbed in frequent pangs of guilt over all that I had missed along the way.

Yes, Avantika was gone! Where? I didn't know.

Wait, the pilot has just announced our descent into Delhi, the city where she probably is. So, let me quickly fill you in on the events leading up to my travel, and subsequently we shall return to my past and Avantika. For now, the only pertinent fact is that in the short span of eight months, Avantika had become an inseparable part of our lives – Myra's and mine – and her presence had become a habit, a necessity we both couldn't do without.

'You know Rahul; life is too beautiful to be drowned in sorrows. You must get a grip on yourself and put up a brave face, If not for your own self, then for Myra. And for me,' she had said.

It was sometime in the night – I can't recall the exact time. Myra had gone to bed, put to sleep by Avantika. Avantika had arrived in Mumbai the same morning. Her return flight was scheduled for the next day and she was staying over, not the first time of course. We were in the one-bedroom flat in Borivali, a distant suburb of Mumbai, which I had rented out a few months back. The flat was no match for the one in Juhu we had been occupying earlier. Hell, this one didn't even have a balcony, let alone an unobstructed view of the rambling sea that Myra had so grown used to.

When Avantika was staying with us, she and Myra would

share the bedroom while I would be forced to make do with a make-shift bed on the floor of the hall. It was in the hall that I was sitting pensively, clutching a glass brimming with rum and cola. I had made a drink for her too which she had picked up once she emerged after putting Myra to sleep.

She was still nursing her first drink whereas I was on my fourth. Or was it the fifth?

Not a word had been exchanged between us for both of us realised the gravity of the situation staring us in the face. Then suddenly she placed her hand over mine and broke the silence with her words. I could only nod in return.

'I don't know about you, but Myra and you mean the world to me and it pains me immensely to see you like this,' she added. I was amazed at the effortlessness of her statement. She had simply, as a matter of fact, stated something that I had been aching to hear but never had the courage to seek out. I looked up, into her eyes, and saw a maze of emotions that left me in little doubt that she meant every word that she had spoken. Instinctively, I reached out and hugged her. She reciprocated by wrapping her arms around me, and we remained like that, frozen in the moment, for what seemed like eternity.

Then abruptly, she withdrew and rushed back into the bedroom. I called out to her, whispered actually, for the fear of disturbing Myra's sleep, but she did not turn back and I did not pursue her. She had mustered the courage to speak her heart out and if she needed some time alone to come to terms with it, I had no business denying her that.

After many days, I slept in peace that night.

Come morning, everything appeared to have returned to normal, as though the conversation from last night had never actually happened. Avantika kissed Myra goodbye, hugged me and dragging her trolley bag, headed to the door. Abruptly she turned, as though struck by an afterthought, and said to me, 'I intend to take leave from work and stay back in Delhi for some time. So, it might be a few days before you get to see me again. Don't worry about me or about anything else. Everything will be alright.'

Her words hadn't sounded odd to me then, but now, when I think back, there was a sense of unspeakable gloom to them, one that I had failed to notice. Or perhaps, I am overanalysing once again, an after-effect of having had a burgeoning career in consulting not very long back.

Anyway, that was the last I saw of Avantika. She did not call back and neither did she ever visit us. A day went by, and two, and then three and our patience began to wear, especially Myra's. It was at Myra's behest that I tried to reach her on her mobile phone, but to no avail. The phone was switched off.

Over the next few days I kept trying her number, the gap between two attempts diminishing as the hours went by, only to be informed each time by an irritatingly mechanical voice that the number I was attempting to reach was switched off. By now I was beginning to get worried as well. Where had she suddenly disappeared? If she was merely taking a break in Delhi, she should have been available over the phone. And if she had decided to take a road-trip to an unconnected location, she could at least have called and informed me.

It was then that the thought struck me: the only details pertaining to Avantika I had were her name, her place of work, the city she stayed in and her mobile number. I didn't know anything else about her. Not an alternate number I could reach her on and neither a name - a friend or a family member -I could look up and seek help from to figure out her whereabouts.

Avantika, I knew, detested the very concept of social networking and despite her having claimed that she didn't have a profile on any such sites, I tried locating her online. The results turned out just as I had anticipated. Avantika had never shared anything with us – neither with me and nor with Myra – a realisation that was enough to send my thoughts spiralling once again. Was her disappearance pre-meditated? If yes, why? There was nothing she stood to gain by befriending my daughter or me and leaving us in lurch by vanishing abruptly. Why then would she not even bother to inform us of her whereabouts?

It was in that desperate moment that I called her employers – the airline – who were obviously apprehensive of divulging information about one of their employees. Next I landed up at their office, Myra in tow, demanding to know where Avantika was. When asked about my relationship with her, I was left tongue-tied and as a result, following a prompting from the office manager, I was gently ushered out by a security guard with menacing looks and moustaches to match.

I was snorting away my fury, ignoring Myra's pesky questions and nearly dragging her out of the complex when a voice made me pause mid-step.

'Excuse me,' she said. 'Are you a friend of Avantika's?' She was wearing the airline uniform, a hint enough that she was Avantika's colleague and hopefully a well-meaning one. Obviously the commotion I had caused within the office hadn't gone unnoticed and she had shadowed me on my way out.

'Yes,' I said, turning to face her and pulling my eyebrows upwards quizzically.

'Can we step out of the gate if you don't mind?' The ring of conspiracy was obvious in her tone and I took a step back, gesturing for her to lead the way. She led me to a nearby roadside tea stall and ignoring the fascinating glares her tight-fitting dress was drawing from other customers, ordered two cutting chai. She didn't bother to check if I wished to have tea at all or whether Myra too wanted some.

Handing one glass to me and holding the other between her palms, she began, 'I am Neetu, a colleague of Avantika's and

if I am not mistaken, this must be Myra, and you her father.'
So, Avantika had been talking to her colleagues about me… err,
about us. Not bad! I felt a smile emerge on my lips as I affirmed
her supposition with a nod.

'I heard your argument with the office manager and thought
I must share with you whatever little I know. These guys can
become extremely unreasonable at times, you know,' she said,
referring to the manager's irrationality.

'Avantika has not reported to work for about two weeks now.
As per our policies, if an employee is absconding for a week without
any intimation to the office, we try and get in touch with their
family. I believe someone from HR (Human Resources) did try to
get in touch with her family at the Delhi address we have on our
records, but only to discover that it was a rented accommodation
where she stayed alone. The door to the flat was locked and they
had to return empty-handed.'

This was beginning to get even more mysterious now. After
assimilating whatever she had said, I looked back at Neetu. She
was nearly done with her tea. I hadn't even touched mine.

'Thank you, Neetu, for making the effort of sharing this
information with me. But can I ask you for one more favour?
Would it be possible for you to get the address that is on your
company's records? This sudden disappearance is very unlike
Avantika and I am beginning to get concerned about her. If I can
get hold of her address, I could try to trace her on my own.'

Neetu turned out to be more humane than her manager
and agreed to help me instantly. The same evening – yesterday
actually – she mailed me Avantika's Delhi address. And here I
was, landing in her city to find her and hopefully take her back
with me forever.

Two

The city of Delhi can be most cruel and unreasonable to visitors when it intends to, and sadly I had become a willing subject of this brutality.

The pre-paid cab I had hailed at the airport, a rickety apparatus which would have been more effective in mixing cement than ferrying passengers, broke down on the way and I was forced to hail an auto-rickshaw to take me to Munirka Vihar. If the airline records were anything to go by, it was in Munirka Vihar that Avantika had been staying. I did ask the driver for a refund, but the astonished look he returned was enough for me to keep my hope in check. 'I am not the one asking you to leave the taxi. You can wait till the vehicle is fixed and I will drop you to your destination,' he said, shrugging his shoulders helplessly. I was in no state to argue, so I got out without a protest.

I thought my luck had suddenly switched shades, for despite the horror stories I had heard about the Delhi autowallahs, I found a willing one who agreed to take me to my destination and charge me by the meter. It was only when I had seen the India Gate, Parliament House and several other prominent landmarks of the city and the meter reading had well surpassed the amount I had originally paid for the taxi that I came to terms with the ploy responsible for revitalising my luck. I confronted the driver, only to be fed some lame excuse about having taken a circuitous route to avoid traffic. But perhaps the confrontation worked, as within the next ten minutes, he dropped me at the gate of Munirka Vihar without any further sightseeing detours.

Munirka Vihar was a well-kept complex of three-storeyed, white buildings, located in the southern part of Delhi, in reasonable proximity to the domestic airport, a fact I discovered only later. The security guard was not at the gate, so I walked straight in, surveying the numbers stencilled on the buildings to guide me to Avantika's flat. It was one of the four flats (Numbere203) on the second floor of Building 'D' and a padlock stared back at me, just as I had already been informed.

I surveyed the other three doors and with no particular thought in my mind, reached out for the call-bell adjacent to one of them. Neighbours can sometimes serve as a source for more information than one can imagine and my mind was made to tap each of them for whatever they could tell me about Avantika. I had to start somewhere, and from where I stood, one door looked as inviting or uninviting as the other.

As my fingers pressed the button, I heard lines of a popular devotional number play out in the distance. The improvised bell permitted the lines to repeat twice before stopping, a little after which I heard footsteps approaching the door. The door opened just enough to let a head out from the crack, and the head of a middle-aged lady, a liberal streak of vermillion adorning the partition of her predominantly black hair, emerged from it. She didn't say anything, just stared at me with a look that made me feel as if I had just descended from outer space, if not escaped from a well-guarded cage of the Delhi zoo.

'Hi, I am Rahul, a friend of Avantika's – the girl who stays here,' I addressed her, pointing to the locked door behind me. 'Avantika has not been coming to work for the past fortnight and she is not reachable on her mobile either. I thought maybe you could provide me some information that might help me in locating her,' I added.

The stare persisted, her face blank, as though I had addressed her in Mandarin and not Hindi, and then, suddenly she withdrew and slammed the door at me. Her haste was reminiscent of the times that my ex-wife remembered about the forgotten pot of milk she had left on the stove to boil. She hadn't spoken a word, not even a change of expressions, before slamming the door on me. For a moment I stood there, transfixed, trying to figure the part of my dialogue that might have offended her. I failed to come up with any.

Brushing away the initial setback, I shifted my focus to the door adjacent to Mrs. I-don't-talk-to-strangers. This time a man in his early sixties, clad in white kurta-payjama, appeared in response to the bell. He presented himself in full, not concealing any part of him from my view, and even nodded his head to my introduction. I felt optimistic. Call me chauvinistic if you may, but the sight of a fellow male suddenly made me believe in the prevalence of logic and reason, but maybe I had presumed too much too soon.

'Tell me Mr. Rahul, have you obtained the society's permission to go about this door-to-door campaign of yours?' he shot out, shattering any illusions of empathy and understanding that his initial bearing might have resulted in.

'Society?'

'Yes, the housing society. You can't just barge in and go about knocking people's doors, you know. And how did the guard permit you inside in the first place? Did you tell him what you were planning to do?' he continued with his assault.

'Sir, I rang your bell only because you are Avantika's neighbour and I thought you might be able to help me find her. I am not going about any door-to-door canvassing here. And I didn't come across any guard on my way up to her flat,' I said, unaware that in the heat of the moment I might have dug a grave for the poor, though somewhat irresponsible, guard.

The man excused himself, asking me to wait where I was, and I obliged. I wasn't some thief, robber or even a door-to-door salesman, and I certainly wasn't going to allow him to trample all over me just like that. For a moment my heart went out to Avantika for the kind of people she was surrounded with, but my thoughts were quickly steered back to the present. From inside I could hear the man screaming at someone. He had probably managed to catch the guard on the intercom.

'The guard is on his way up,' he announced, returning to the door after audibly slamming down the receiver. I glared at him viciously. I could have sliced him into two if I could help. What if the guard was on his way up, was I supposed to tremble in fear or fall down at his feet? I allowed my rage to surface on my face and he was quick to avert his gaze.

Soon enough a plump, unkempt man came huffing and puffing up the stairs and the old man exploded like a firecracker on sighting him. I remained a silent spectator as he disparaged the guard for his absence from the assigned post, threatening not only to claim his job, but to starve his children, wife and even his deceased ancestors to death. The guard listened, his head bowed slightly, but not an anxious twitch on his face. This must be common fare for him, I assumed.

'Sir, please come,' he muttered, looking at me with expectant eyes once the old man was done with the dressing down. Somewhat embarrassed at what he had had to endure, partly because of me, I quietly followed him down the stairs.

'*Chutiya hai sala*! One of these days he will scream his heart to a stop and no one will even take him to the hospital. He will die a dog's death, the bastard,' the guard spoke once we were safely out of the building. I couldn't help but smile.

Seizing the opportunity, I engaged the man in small talk and he turned out to be as responsive and eager as a doe in heat. It was from him I learnt that the man we had just walked away from was a widower, Raman *Saheb*, who was an acknowledged menace among the residents of Munirka Vihar. From parked cars to playing children, the man had problems with just about everything. Which is why, Tiwari, the guard, thought his children and grandchildren seldom came down to visit him.

Quickly I steered the discussion towards Avantika and asked him if he knew anything that might help me find her.

'The Didi from D-203, she is a marvellous girl,' he began his discourse. I did not attempt to hurry him. 'Always gives us a decent *baksheesh* during festivals, and every now and then she also gives chocolates and biscuits for our children. Otherwise, in today's world who thinks about us poor people, *Saheb*, tell me?'

I don't know whether his statement was meant to drop a hint, but I pulled out two crisp hundred rupee notes and placed them in his palm, wrapping his fingers over them with my other hand. 'This wasn't needed, really,' he said, even as he pocketed the money.

'Usually a company car comes to pick her up and she doesn't return for a day or two. She flies in a plane to other cities. Airhostess, I think that is what they call her. However, this time round I haven't seen her for a while... ten-twelve days at least,' he offered.

'When was the last time you saw her?' I pressed on.

Despite his best efforts, he could not recall the exact date when he had last seen Avantika, but he conceded that she could only have departed in the company car, for if she had left in another vehicle he would have noticed. 'But I have had morning shifts this entire month. She could have left during the night too and if you wish, I can check with the other guard, the one who does the night shifts,' he offered.

Authorising him to seek whatever information he could from the other guard, I asked him if he knew a way I could get inside Avantika's flat. 'I might come across a clue that could help me find her,' I said, appealing to the concern I had seen in his eyes for Avantika and topping it with the promise of a 'healthy' reward.

He reached out for a dilapidated registered covered with random scrawling and began flipping through its pages. It would be a miracle if he found whatever it was that he was looking for in there, I thought. And miraculously indeed, he turned to me and said, 'Shyam Sharma, he is the owner of D-203. Here, this is his phone number. He stays somewhere in Vasant Vihar. A friendly sort of a fellow, he should have a duplicate set of keys and might be able to help you get inside the flat.'

Taking the piece of paper on which Tiwari had scribbled Shyam Sharma's number, I stepped away from the gate and took out my mobile phone. With Sharma, my search for the one sensible and rational soul on the streets of Delhi ended. He not only sounded civil and educated, but also expressed concern over Avantika's sudden disappearance. 'Last I had seen her was about two months back when she had called me for some plumbing work that needed to be done in the flat. She usually transfers the rent to my bank account within the first few days of each month and this month also the rent was transferred on time,' he volunteered.

'Mr. Sharma, I was wondering if you would have a set of duplicate keys to the flat. There might be something inside to tell us where she might be,' I appealed.

There was a moment's hesitation before he replied. 'Young man, please don't get me wrong, but it wouldn't be appropriate for me to open the door in Avantika's absence. I am not questioning your intentions, but till such time that I keep getting my rent, I have no business opening the flat to anyone but her. I am a retired man and I try to keep away from such hassles as far as I can help.'

Mr. Sharma's rationality – one that I had just been thanking my stars for - had suddenly emerged as a barrier and I found myself unable to think of a valid counter to offer. So I requested him, pleading almost, to not let his principles stand in the way of finding a girl who might be in who-knows-what trouble. His ensuing silence meant that my words were hitting home and I persisted till he eventually spoke.

'Why don't you speak to the police? If she has been missing for over two weeks, you must certainly file a complaint with them. It will be in her best interest as well, since it might not be possible for you to cover all bases on your own. And the presence of the cops will take care of my inhibitions in opening the door to the flat as well,' he said.

I could have persisted with my attempts to convince him, but I suddenly saw merit in his suggestion. The thought of approaching the police had not even occurred to me and come to think of it, it now seemed like the most reasonable thing to do. In fact somewhere at the back of my mind I had been hoping that I would find Avantika chilling out at home with some arbitrary reason, her phone getting lost for instance, to explain the lack of communication. It was wishful thinking I knew, and now that it had turned out to be just that, it was about time the experts were called upon.

Concluding my conversation with Mr. Sharma, I returned to the Munirka Vihar gate where I could see Tiwari eyeing me curiously. A better part of the day had already gone by, leaving me with absolutely nothing, and I could see the sun rapidly descending down the horizon. I asked Tiwari for some reasonably priced stay options in the vicinity and the directions to the nearest police station. Armed with both pieces of information, I hailed an auto to the Munirka Police Station, keeping an eye on the road for any undesired detours the ambitious driver might wish to embark upon.

It was certain now; I would have to stay back in Delhi for the night. There was little additional ground I could expect to cover in whatever remained of the day. While in the auto, struggling to make myself heard over its constant spurting and chugging, I called Myra to update her of my plans and the near-nothing I had managed to uncover about her Avantika Aunty's whereabouts.

I had left her in the custody of my cousin Rashmi. Rashmi had a son a few years older than Myra and they stayed not very far (by Mumbai standards) from where I did – three stations on the local train line to be precise. Since the time of my divorce, I had availed Rashmi's help on several occasions to look after Myra while I was travelling on work. Myra too looked forward to spending time with them, a welcome and lively change to what our own house had to offer to her.

It was Rashmi who took my call and once I had briefed her about the need for my extended stay in Delhi, she passed the handed phone over to Myra.

'Did you find Avantika Aunty, Papa?' were her first words. It pained me from within to burst her bubble of hope. I told her that I was staying back and that I would certainly find Avantika, no matter what it took. 'Please do find her papa,' she somberly responded, sounding exceedingly mature for a girl of five years. I wanted to continue talking to her, reassure her and fuel my own resolve to locate Avantika with her yearning, but the auto had come to a halt and I could see a board reading 'Munirka Police Station' ahead of me.

It was a small single-floor structure with an elaborate lawn, a boundary wall and a metal gate – a luxury considering the prime real estate the station stood on. There were rickety jeeps and motorbikes parked in the open space and conspicuous-looking men lolled about in twos and threes, conversing in hushed and cautious tones.

Ignoring them, I walked towards the steps leading to a large wooden door above which was another tin board with 'Munirka Police Station' painted in block letters. As if anyone would come inside looking for the Scotland Yard offices even if he or she happened to have missed the large board hanging over the main gate. The door was slightly ajar and I was pleasantly surprised at the sight that presented itself.

I had entered a large hall where two policemen sat on separate desks talking to people and registering their complaints. Or so it appeared at least, given the ferocity with which they were scribbling into their registers. Lining one of walls were a series of metallic benches where five people sat, four men and a woman, waiting for their turns to put up their grievances before the authorities. The hall was spic-and-span and appeared systematic and immaculate unlike the commonly held perception about inside of a police station.

A passage broke away from the hall, turning to where, I assumed, the real police-work happened – third degree tortures and planning for the next set of raids. Flanking the passage were two wooden doors with plates affixed to the adjacent walls proclaiming the names and designations of the occupants. These were the senior officers who were possibly at the helm of affairs here. Having surveyed the surroundings, I deposited myself on the bench, as far away from my fellow complainants as I could, waiting for my turn.

After about half an hour, one of the policemen summoned me to his desk by a shake of the ball-point pen he held between his fingers. The five people waiting before me – two groups of three and two respectively – had been dealt with and the bench was now brimming with a fresh set of faces.

'I need to file a Missing Persons Report,' I said, taking one of the two seats on my side of the desk. The policeman, who had once again begun scribbling on his register, looked up, amazed, as though my voice had sounded to him like that of a long time dead relative.

Satbir Gahlaut, as his name-plate suggested, was a thickset man with a fleshy, nondescript face. His suspicious little eyes, a funny pair for his well-rounded face, sized me up before he spoke in a shrilling, petulant tone.

'What do you guys think, we have nothing better to do out here but track your wives who keep running away with their boyfriends?' I was aghast. His apathy was appalling. And while I was still recovering from the shock, he barked once again. 'Who is missing?'

Eyeing him suspiciously, I began narrating whatever I knew about Avantika's disappearance. Mr. Gahlaut clearly wasn't a man known for his patience and kept interrupting my dialogue with a flurry of questions, grimacing at whatever I said in return: Where does she hail from? How do you know her? What is your relationship with her? Where are her parents? Why haven't they come to the station?

I must admit, I didn't have particularly satisfactory answers to all his queries, but the fact was that a girl was missing and it was part of Satbir's job to help locate her. So, when he dropped his pen on the table, clasping his palms to rest his chin over them and addressed me, I found myself burning with agitation, like an egg left to boil for too long.

'She is a grown up girl and free to go wherever she wishes. If she chooses not to inform you of her whereabouts, that's your problem, not mine. Stop wasting my time and get back to where you have come from,' he said. His tone wasn't particularly high-pitched but it was menacing nonetheless and his tapering eyes, boring into mine, lent him an extremely intimidating look.

'You mean you are not going to register my complaint?' I shot back. By now I was simmering with rage and had to try exceedingly hard to control my voice.

'You heard me.'

'There is a girl missing for God's sake, for over a fortnight now. How can you say that you will not register a complaint? It is your duty, you will have to record it,' I shot back.

'Funny, but somehow I don't feel that I will 'have' to do anything you say,' he returned, a contemptuous smile emerging on his face. 'And if you don't get your sorry ass out of here in a flash I will personally engrave it in a manner that you will find it hard to sit on a chair for the rest of your fucking life.'

I did not make any attempt to get up, but by the looks of him, Satbir was more than capable of doing what he claimed. I had to be careful in how I tackled him. I was still weighing my words when he shifted his gaze and sprung from his seat as though it had suddenly grown thorns. For a second I was startled. I thought he was going to punch me across the table. But, his right hand went up and touched the side of his forehead in a salute. At about the same time I felt a hand on my shoulder.

Startled once again, I turned around to find another policeman standing behind and looking straight at me. Judging by the stars on his uniform and the manner in which Satbir had risen to greet him, he had to be a senior officer. He was a smart fellow, fit, without the quintessential cop-paunch, and roughly my own age. His face looked vaguely familiar, but I couldn't instantly recall as to where I had last seen him.

'Rahul?' he spoke.

His voice was a dead giveaway and recognising him, I shot up from the chair, turning to face him.

'Anand? Is that you? Wow, is this a coincidence or what?' He smiled back, patting both my shoulders and eyeing me from top to bottom. I would have hugged him, not so much because of the long interval we were meeting after, but for the time and place he had chosen to turn up. If it wasn't for him, Mr. Gahlaut could have been battering me to pulp just then. However, not meaning to embarrass him in the presence of his subordinates, I decided against the embrace.

'Come,' he said, gesturing towards one of the rooms that opened into the hall. 'Anand Kumar – I.P.S.' the plaque outside the door read.

Anand and I went back a long way, to our high-school days in Pune. Back then he wasn't quite the spirited cop he appeared to be now. He was a small-town boy from somewhere in Madhya Pradesh, if my memory doesn't fail me, who had come wedded to his books, nurturing a dream of investing his student years in making a career for himself.

I, on the other hand, was the local boy – one who had many friends, was aware of the local hang-outs and knew how to lead life king-size. It was this contrast in our personalities that had brought us close. For the two years that we were together, we remained the best of buddies, complimenting each other like blazing fire does to placid water. I would look to him for class notes, tutorials and reminders for pending assignment submissions and in turn, whenever I could manage, I would drag him to join in our carousing and social jaunts.

And then the inevitable happened. Anand got admission in a prestigious college of the Delhi University and left Pune in favour of the larger metropolis for the sake of his dreams. We remained in touch for a while and then time and our respective preoccupations took their toll, drawing us apart, leaving each into the world he had chosen for himself.

For once, it appeared that fate had decided to side with me. What else could explain the sudden appearance of Anand after almost a decade-and-half, at a police station in Delhi that I otherwise would never have imagined visiting, and on a day when I could do with his help like a dying man could do with a shot of morphine?

Once we were seated, Anand rang for coffee and we began sharing notes on the time gone by. He, I learnt, had settled down in Delhi and was putting up in a government flat in R.K. Puram (wherever that was) with his wife and two kids. I updated him about the happenings in my life too, a drastically abridged version, since I didn't wish to spend the entire evening sharing my uninspiring story. After about half an hour had passed, he brushed the topic I had been waiting for, casually, as though it were an extended segment of our catching up.

'So, what brings you here?' he asked.

I began telling him about Avantika, how she had suddenly vanished and the efforts that had already been made by her employers and me in trying to locate her. He had questions too, not very dissimilar to his subordinate's, but I found comfort in that fact that he was listening intently to my explanations.

After listening to my story, he explained how police stations were measured on the prevailing crime rate within their jurisdiction – a seemingly flawed system, he admitted, which often acted as a deterrent to cases being registered, sometimes even those that merited a police enquiry.

'Let's face it, there is a possibility that Avantika has left for someplace on her own, and for reasons best known to her, did not feel the need to inform her employers or even you. There is no conclusive evidence yet that her disappearance has resulted from something out of the ordinary,' he began after a brief contemplative pause.

'Let us do this, give me a day to investigate the case at my level, and depending on what we come across we can decide on whether a formal complaint needs to be filed or not. God willing, we might discover that she is chilling out somewhere in the Himalayas and you, sitting here, are getting all worked up over nothing,' he added. His words were reassuring and I knew that if Anand was saying he would investigate, he would do all in his capacity to find Avantika.

Once I had nodded my consent, he asked me for her address. I gave him both, the address and her landlord's phone number, which he scribbled in a notepad on his desk. When I offered to join him during his visit to Munirka Vihar, he said that he would go there sometime tomorrow, after he had conducted some basic enquiries through his 'regular channels', and that I could accompany him if I so wished. After noting down the other details I was in a position to provide – her mobile number and the name of her employers – he asked, 'Would you have a recent photograph of hers?'

'I will have a few on my laptop, but I haven't carried it along. I could arrange to have some of them e-mailed to you if you want,' I replied.

'Never mind, I will ask for them if the need does arise. And stop worrying yourself to death. We will find her soon enough,' he said, placing his hand on my shoulder reassuringly. 'Where are you putting up in Delhi anyway?' he added.

When I told him that I would be putting up in a hotel, he would hear none of it and insisted that I stay over at his place. My mind was thoroughly screwed, and pathetic as I may sound, I was in no mood to socialise with his wife and children right now. All I needed was a bed where I could lay in peace and get a grip on my thoughts. It was therefore with significant difficulty and a promise to pay him a visit on my next trip that I managed to convince him, albeit reluctantly, to excuse me this time round.

Thanking him for his help and asking him to call me if he came across anything of relevance, I took his leave. I was just about stepping out of the door when he called out to me once again.

'You might not know much about Avantika's life, but has she ever mentioned about someone who might have reasons to nurse a grudge against her? Or, someone who might have a compelling reason to orchestrate her disappearance?'

His words rang like a bell in my head, opening doors that were hitherto hidden from the scope of my contemplations. I turned on my heels, and walking back towards him, said, 'Actually, there is someone who might have both a reason and the wherewithal to do something of that sort.'

'Who?' he returned, a curtain of curiosity falling over his face.

'Shalini, my ex-wife,' I replied, depositing myself once again on the chair I had just left. I knew that I could not leave the room until I shared with Anand the basis for the suspicion that his words had aroused within me.

Three

Time has steadfastly stirred along, as it ever so doggedly does, and the day I first met Shalini is now only a fading mural on the walls of my memories. Almost a dozen summers have passed and yet I can't be sure if Shalini was a blessing or a mistake that I am fated to rue for as long as I live.

It was nearly a month since I had shifted to Andheri, a bustling Mumbai suburb, and was sharing a rented two-bedroom accommodation with three other boys. We were all newly admitted students to a nearby management institute, one that wasn't likely to make it to any of the top-ten rankings, unless there happened to be one published by some or the other fashion magazine, with glamour as the sole defining criteria for pre-eminence.

Though the institute did not have an on-campus hostel, it did provide accommodation assistance by bunching together sets of students and helping them find rental apartments through a network of registered brokers. And this was how I had found myself sharing the flat and two extremely crucial years of my life with Fuddu, Poka and Battery.

No, their parents merited no credit for the ingenious names they had been festooned with. It was the institute that was responsible. A warped tradition called for seniors to name the *Fucchas* (as the fresh-men were called) based on perceptions they gathered over the untimely ragging sessions that went on for the first few weeks of every new batch joining the campus. While the other two were named solely on account of their external appearances, Poka's name had a history to it that not many were in the know of.

One day when a bunch of us were in the canteen, trying to make sense of the assignments we had been bombarded with without a warning, a couple of seniors approached us. After the customary round of introductions, one of them, the sleazy-faced one, asked us to share our most unique sexual escapades. The best story, it was declared, will be rewarded and the narrator would be allowed to walk out of the canteen unharmed. Considering that a win would enable one of us to make good his escape, a sense of competition was quick to emerge and we began telling our stories, liberally sprucing it up with our fantasies and imagination.

Poka, or Ajit, as he was known till that fateful day, began telling us a story of how, back in his hometown, he had been making out with a mother-daughter duo for an uninterrupted stretch of over six months. Each one unaware of Poka's ongoing transactions with the other, of course! The girl had been his classmate, he explained, who was blessed with a mother who looked more like her elder sister. The girl wasn't bad-looking either and therefore Ajit had befriended her, visiting her house every now and then on some or the other pretext. He also made it a point to shower his friend's mother with compliments, harmless words of appreciation, whenever he came to face her – out of sheer habit, he claimed.

One day on a casual visit to the friend's house, he learnt (from her mother of course) that the girl was out shopping and when the mother offered to make him some tea, he couldn't refuse. The girl's absence did not deter him from his flirtatious ways and to his utter amazement he found that 'Aunty' was not only responding to the words, but also egging him on with her retorts.

One thing led to another and before Ajit could realise, he was in bed, doing to the mother what he had long desired to do to the daughter, but hadn't succeeded till then. It was however only a matter of time that the girl too succumbed to his advances and thence began the story that was to shield him from a certain bout of ragging in a college canteen of a distant city many months later.

The seniors, like the rest of us, listened to his account in utter amazement and when Ajit was done with his narration, there was an unmistakable hint of awe in the looks they gave him. It was this self-proclaimed proficiency in the art of poking that earned him the nickname Poker. And eventually, ease of articulation transformed it to its present form – Poka.

By virtue of being his roommate, it took me little time to realise that the basis for his name hadn't been entirely unfounded. Within a span of four weeks two girls from the institute, one a senior and the other from our own class, had visited our flat and left after spending about an hour each behind closed doors with Poka. On both occasions Poka had forewarned us and we, the unfortunate trio, had to evacuate the house, allowing him the privacy he needed. It was tough, straining our imagination to reconstruct the scenes unfolding within the flat and letting out despairing sighs, but this was an unwritten code that all men who have ever shared a dwelling will swear by, and there was no way we were going to challenge it.

Poka wasn't an exceptional sight, just an average-looking boy, like the hundreds you come across during a short walk through any of the city streets. But he had the gift of gab. He could talk himself out of any unwarranted situation, and when it came to girls, he could talk them into any situation he wanted.

Coming back to the day I had first met Shalini. It was early on a Saturday morning and I was still in bed when a sudden commotion in the room woke me up. Rubbing my eyes with the back of my hand, I got up to discover that Poka had returned from his jogging, a fad he had recently acquired and, I was sure, he wasn't likely to stick with for long. It was usual for him to make a *tornado-esque* entrance, but today he appeared overly excited. Like he had found a pot of gold at the end of the rainbow or, knowing Poka's preferences, had been pounced upon by a gang of cougars.

'Get up sleepy head… and listen to this… You bums must have seriously done something nice in your past lives for God to send me as your saviour,' he announced self-indulgently.

'What?' I shot back annoyed. Whatever it was that he meant to tell me, it couldn't have been worth my while. Probably, just a load of garbage for which he had pulled me out of my sleep.

'Don't look as if I have robbed you of something. We are going for a movie in the evening… a date,' he said, exhibiting his dentures. I didn't know whether he expected me to fall on his feet or something, but he seemed somewhat taken aback when, disinterested, I rolled on the bed to turn my face away from him.

But once Poka got going, there was no stopping him. I was made to hear the entire story despite all my vocal protests. How he saw a couple of pretty girls brisk-walking on the jogging track which encircled our apartment complex, how he initiated conversation with them and how he convinced them to join us for a movie the same evening. I could only empathise with the girls. I was certain that their commitment to the date was only a ploy to get Poka off their backs and that we were placing ourselves to be stood-up. However, I was proven wrong.

Come evening, we went down to the complex gate, Poka eventually begging me into joining him when none of his I-am-doing-you-a-favour antics worked. A few minutes were still left for the designated time of our meeting when we saw the girls emerge from the building behind the one we stayed in, not two but three of them. Judging by Poka's looks, he hadn't expected the third girl to be there. But he was quick to recover.

'Hi Shalini', he said, extending his hand and a 100-watt smile to the girl wearing denims and a black tank top. She was a sight alright, curvaceous, not too tall, but fair with spotless skin and features that made you want to cuddle her instantly.

'Hey,' she replied, breaking into a smile of her own. Poka went on to greet the other girl, the one who had probably been accompanying Shalini when he had met them and whose name he had obviously forgotten, and introduced himself to the third one before coming alive to my existence. 'This is Rahul,' he offered, thankfully referring to me by my real name and not the proxy plastered upon me by the dim-witted seniors.

What? I haven't told you my nickname yet? Well, I am not divulging that either? As some wise advertisers have said, '*Itna paisa me itna hi milenga* (This is all you get for the money you have paid).' But to curb your curiosity, let me tell you that if the name were to be mentioned on national television, it would have to be dubbed with a beep.

So, coming back to the girls, we learnt that they were all from Delhi and had taken up a flat on rent in the same complex as ours. While Shalini and Ishita had come to Mumbai recently and were pursuing a course in Fashion Designing, Prerna, the eldest of the lot, was working for a television channel. It was only Shalini and Ishita that Poka had originally invited for the movie. His brazen advances must have scared them into bringing along a chaperone in Prerna, I mused. Then I smiled to myself. One chaperone or two, they were not safe in Poka's company even if they had come with an entire battalion of bodyguards.

Poka was on the job from the word go. He was brazenly flirting with Shalini and all through the movie one could hear the buzz of whispers being exchanged between the two. Once the movie was over, we decided to grab a bite at a nearby fast-food joint. We had placed our orders and were waiting at the table when Poka, his voice dripping with honey, asked Shalini if he could read her hand. Poka often turned into an expert chierologist at the sight of a pretty girl. He claimed that it was the best way to arouse curiosity in them and to sample first-hand what their touch felt like.

'Sure you can,' she said, extending her hand towards him. And in the same breath she added, 'I hope you realise though, that this ploy is as dated as the time when women wore knickers. I don't know if it has worked for you in the past, but just so you are not disappointed later, let me warn you that feeling my hands is all you are going to manage.'

All of us burst out laughing at her statement and Poka suddenly dropped her hand and withdrew his own, as if he had touched fire. A flustered shade of red emerged on his face and he fell back on the chair.

I don't know the reason behind Shalini's sudden rebuke of Poka, perhaps his dogged persistence had worn out her patience or maybe she was like that only, forthright and straight. But the act had suddenly lifted her by a couple of pedestals in my eyes. No, It wasn't because I was jealous of Poka or something – if anything, I felt bad for his momentary discomfiture, even though, knowing Poka, I was certain that he would bounce back in no time. it was because this was the first time I had seen a girl thwart his advances so ruthlessly. Her act was awe-inspiring and just then I felt a reverence towards Shalini that I had never felt for any other girl.

I wasn't very far from reality in assuming that Poka would return to being his normal self soon. Even before dinner was served, he was back chit-chatting with the girls and dropping compliments, a dime a dozen. Only, now his focus had shifted slightly, from Shalini to Ishita, and I could see her blushing in wake of the newfound admirer. Well, each one to their own, I thought, smiling once again as I recalled the look on Poka's face from barely a few moments ago.

Once we had returned from the movie and I was back in my bed, I found myself thinking about Shalini. I knew I was being stupid. A girl who had dealt with Poka's advances so severely would, in all likelihood, make mincemeat out of me. But my thoughts seemed to have acquired a mind of their own and kept darting back, no matter how hard I tried to steer them clear of her.

'So, you have suddenly developed a liking for jogging. I hope this doesn't have anything to do with the last evening?' Poka jibed, watching me tie my shoelaces the next morning. I was up and ready for the exercise even before he had opened his eyes.

It turned out to be a futile exercise, literally. Neither Shalini nor Ishita showed up and I was left huffing and panting, trying to keep pace with an energised Poka. But that was just the first morning. The advantages of residing in the same complex are many and I discovered them when I found myself bumping into Shalini at the strangest of places – near the main gate of the building, at the nearby grocery store, at the auto stand and so on. Whenever we met, we exchanged basic pleasantries and nothing more. Her treatment of Poka had left my courage in shock and it did not permit me to utter even a single word out of its designated place.

However, the more I saw of her, the more permanent her presence within my thoughts became. My mind was now equipped with several images of Shalini – her infectious laughter, her angelic smile, Shalini in the yellow salwar suit and Shalini in her shorts and tees. By now I had even discovered a pattern in their jogging jaunts. It was only three days in a week – Tuesdays, Thursdays and Saturdays – that Shalini and Ishita visited the track, and I began to ensure that I was there to greet them then. In fact Poka wasn't entirely wrong in claiming that it was only on those three days that I found exercise to be a worthwhile vocation. He had even voiced his suspicion that something was brewing between Shalini and me already. I had been quick to dismiss the idea.

Meanwhile Poka appeared to have covered some ground too, with Ishita of course. The manner of their interactions, mounting in intimacy every other time we met as a group, was a certain indication of it. And to settle any doubts that I might have had, it was Poka who told me that the girls had invited us over for dinner. 'Prerna is travelling on work, so she wouldn't be around,' he had added with a wink.

On the designated day we spent ample time in choosing the clothes we would wear, eventually settling for the denims and t-shirts we had both picked up initially. We even bought a bouquet each for the girls, inexpensive and identical, lest the gesture was misconstrued to be yet another attempt to woo them. With a heart fluttering like a frog on steroids, I followed Poka to their building and ambled up the stairway to their flat. While he rested his finger on the doorbell, I recall having said a silent prayer. Now, I wonder why.

It was a small flat, similar in size to the one we were residing in, but made much bigger by the manner in which the girls had done it up. The sitting area in the living room comprised cushion-lined settees, a centre table with neatly arranged magazines on it and two corner lamps which served as the only source of illumination then. The dim lighting and fragrance from the incense that was burning somewhere, away from our immediate vision, gave the hall an exotic look. And to top it were the two girls, looking pretty as ever. Shalini was wearing a loose cotton skirt with a collared t-shirt, simple yet elegant, and for a moment I struggled to take my eyes away from her.

'What will you drink?' Ishita asked as soon as we were ushered inside and seated on the settees.

'Beer or Rum with Cola, whatever you have would be fine,' Poka replied. I was glad that he spoke before I did. In my head I was still debating between a glass of water and a cup of tea to call for.

'We have both.'

'Rum then,' he said. 'I will go with Rum as well,' I quickly added.

Ishita nodded and walked to the wooden cabinet sitting ominously in one corner of the room while Shalini proceeded towards the kitchen. The shelf from which Ishita extracted the two bottles - Vodka and Rum respectively - was lined with several bottles of varying shapes and sizes. I was amazed to see such a well-equipped bar in a house inhabited by three single girls. Perhaps my relatively small-town upbringing was to blame, but I couldn't help admiring the guts of the girls. We didn't have half as exciting a collection of alcohol in our flat. It was an entirely different matter that if we did somehow come up with one, the bottles would run the risk of being drained in a single evening, two at the most.

Anyway, soon the centre table was stacked with plates-full of snacks, an ice-bucket and bottles of alcohol and mixers. We began chit-chatting as we sipped our drinks, Vodka for the ladies and Rum for the men. I was feeling good about life, generally. The girls too appeared far more relaxed today than they had during our previous planned meetings. I couldn't tell whether it was the comfort of being on familiar turf or Prerna's absence which was responsible for their amenable demeanour, but I couldn't care less. Just looking at Shalini and hearing her talk left me with little else to desire.

Ishita had refilled our glasses for the third time, to my further surprise, the girls were managing to keep pace with us in draining their glasses too, when she turned to Poka and said, 'Come, I will show you around the house.'

Poka got up, sparing her a smile, one of his I-know-what's-on-your-mind ones. I wasn't invited, so I remained where I was. Shalini too remained seated, sipping on her drink nonchalantly as the two dissolved into the passage leading up to the bedrooms.

It was awkward, the ensuing silence. For the amount of time they were taking inside, they might as well have been painting the house instead of simply looking around. It wasn't a large place and if you listened intently, which, in the absence of anything better to do, I was doing, you could hear the intermittent sighs, moans and ruffle of clothes that emerged from the direction in which Poka and Ishita had disappeared. Both Shalini and I were old enough to figure what was happening inside and that added to the tension in the air, an uneasy nervous kind of tension.

'Would you care for a joint?' she asked, breaking the silence and reaching out for her handbag without waiting for a reply.

Until then I had never ever smoked up. Marijuana to me had been a vice to be kept away from; its mere mention flashing my mind with images of drug-addicts sprawled wretchedly in dingy corners which I remembered from the public service messages played in cinema halls. But then there was the false sense of pride that I needed to contend with. How sissy would I look turning down a smoke offered by a pretty girl?

Shalini dug out a crumpled cigarette, one that appeared polio-stricken with its creased body and tapering anterior, and struck a match to deftly light it. She took a couple of long drags, her eyes shutting in proclamation of the immense pleasure she seemed to be deriving with the smoke hitting her lungs, before passing the stick over to me. I took a measured drag too and instantly burst out coughing.

'No silly,' she said, bursting into a giddy laughter. 'That is not how you do it. Here, let me show you.'

I was somewhat discomfited at my inexperience having shown, but her casual laughter was enough to serve as an immediate ointment. I took to the lessons in smoking a joint with a vigour which, if I had managed to garner during my MBA preparations, would undoubtedly have seen me through to a Harvard or a Wharton. In no time I was smoking like a pro, inhaling the acrid smoke and holding it with my breath till it had transferred its poison into my bloodstream.

Slowly the joint began to have its effect. I felt as if I had been drawn from the scene and turned into a distant spectator instead. Everything in the frame appeared to be moving rather slowly, as if it existed in an entirely different dimension of time. It was a surreal experience and I was relishing it to the hilt.

'You look cute like that... all droopy-eyed and high,' I heard a distant voice say. It took me some time to realise that the words had come from Shalini. Poka and Ishita had not returned by then, I realised. Then, suddenly aware that I might have missed something, I returned to analysing what she had just said. Some more time passed before I could decipher the compliment in my head. Smiling, I looked at her and said, 'Thank you.' She burst out laughing once again.

The recollections I have thereafter are all hazy and abstract, like the contents of a paint tray had been splashed on an empty canvas. It was only when the Bai switched off the fan to sweep the room that I managed to open my eyes. I was lying on my own bed and my head was throbbing like it was an egg ready to hatch. The sun's bright rays were seeping into the room from every little crevice they could find, and yet my lips were stretched in a smile. The fantastic evening had blended into a brand new day and from where I saw it, it appeared to be holding plenty of promise.

The dinner, funnily enough, during the course of which I don't remember having swallowed a single morsel of food, turned out to be just the beginning of times that I had never imagined I would see.

We, Shalini and I, found ourselves settling into a groove running at a slight elevation from the pedestal of normal friendship. Suddenly, items we could spend hours chatting about sprung up from nowhere, objects of common interest like highlights of the day gone by, our aspirations, our dreams, our families, the size of Ruchi Aunty's bra (she was the quintessential nuisance found parading in our otherwise peaceful housing complex) and what was transpiring between Poka and Ishita.

I found myself spending plenty of time in her company and I wasn't exactly complaining. She would call on the intercom asking if I was free to accompany her to the cyber café or the nearby market, and as luck would have it, I was almost always available. I enjoyed when she exercised authority over me, asking (not requesting, mind you) me to do small chores or to escort her someplace. It made me feel wanted. Once when she had taken ill, it was me she summoned to take her to the doctor when either of her roommates would have gladly done the needful. This made me bloat from within and given the miserable state she was in, I had to struggle hard to veil my joy with a curtain of empathetic gloom.

It wasn't just the two of us, Poka and Ishita were also going strong and often the four of us found ourselves drinking and smoking up at either of the two flats, often ours, since both Poka and I were not very comfortable around Prerna.

As for Fuddu and Battery, they had maintained distance from our merrymaking from the very beginning and would usually retire to the room they shared between them when the girls were visiting. And even if either of them was around, their docility and nicety prevented them from inconveniencing us much. If this makes you think that we took the poor souls for granted, well, maybe just an itsy-bitsy bit.

Unlike Poka and Ishita who had surpassed the boundaries of friendship during their very first real meeting, for us it took a lot more time, seven months almost.

Surprisingly, Poka and Ishita's fling was underway even then, a record duration by his own admissions. I take the liberty of terming their relationship a fling purely because of Poka's ways. Since the time he had started seeing Ishita, I had known him to be involved with at least one other girl from the campus, who he had even brought back home on a couple of occasions. I didn't know whether to applaud his guts or to disregard it as his stupidity, but sometimes I couldn't help but wonder as to what would happen if Ishita were to drop by while he was busy entertaining the other girl. Luck, I had heard, had a way of running out on people. But in case of Poka it appeared to have made an exception. He never got caught.

It was Shalini's birthday, second November; I can never forget the date. She had thrown a 'small' party and both Poka and I were on the list of invitees. The venue was a lounge-bar in Andheri and when we arrived at the venue, we realised that what she had referred to as a small gathering actually had over fifty people in attendance. She must have invited the whole of her fashion designing class, I thought, trying to work out an estimate of the amount it would set her back by. The number I came up with made my eyes go wide in disbelief.

We didn't know most of the people there whereas both Shalini and Ishita had their hands full with guests to attend to. Consequently, once we had wished Shalini and handed over the bouquets we were carrying, Poka suggested that we head for the bar and make good our presence. Shrugging my shoulders, I followed him. But Poka was Poka and I should have known better than to believe the drivel that all he had on his mind was alcohol.

There were three girls, pretty looking and all decked up in dresses designed with the very intent of delighting the male eye, resting their backs on the bar counter and surveying the dance floor as they sipped their drinks. They were clearly not a part of Shalini's party, regular patrons of the lounge perhaps. Poka conveyed our order to the barman, 'accidently' brushing against one of the girls, and like the gentleman he was, immediately turning to render an apology. Little did the girls know that the apology (and the slight accident too) was all but a part of Poka's ploy to initiate conversation. And it worked wonders as even before the bartender could return with our drinks, we had already exchanged names and handshakes. Poka was nothing short of a master at his game.

We learnt that the girls worked in the film industry, handling some technical stuff I didn't much care about, but nevertheless a fascinating occupation as far as we outsiders were concerned. No sooner had we got talking that Poka had identified his target, Shauna, a petite girl in a black backless dress, and was brazenly wooing her. Going by the way Shauna was reacting to his cheesy one-liners, most of which I had heard over a million times already, she was undoubtedly relishing the attention too.

Poka's focused approach left me to engage with the other two girls, which I did. Cordially only, mind you, and only because I couldn't suddenly begin to play deaf and mute. I had my eye out for Shalini as well, who appeared busy circulating among the several sets of friends she had managed to accumulate. She looked stunning in her beige tights and emerald green top. Matching earrings were dangling from her ears and the slight touch of make-up, a thing she usually stayed away from, made her look absolutely gorgeous. I was finding it exceedingly difficult to take my eyes off her and focus on the conversation I was in the midst of.

We were discussing, if I recall correctly, the remuneration range for 'extras' who did minor roles in films (I had little doubt that Poka was already scheming about ways to make his pretty face seen on the big screen) when I saw Shalini step towards the dance floor. She was accompanied by a boy, one of those I-am-a-gift-to-womankind types I had noticed earlier as well. He took her hands and they began to dance.

They weren't exactly burning the floor down with their moves and it was all fine till the DJ switched the number. As soon as the music changed, I saw the guy place his palm on Shalini's derriere and she returning the favour by reaching out for his shoulder. It was a pop number for God's sake! Why on earth were they doing a terrible mish-mash of ballroom and salsa steps to it?

As I witnessed his hands explore her body, I felt a vacuum form within my stomach. It was as though some vital organs had been sucked out of me. My face was simmering and my eyes were such that I could evaporate my drink by simply looking at it.

'Come, let's go,' I said abruptly, without even looking at Poka.

'What?' he shot out. There was a look of incredulity in his eyes. 'Are you out of your mind? The party has just about begun,' he added, putting on a pleading smile and flickering his gaze ever so slightly in Shauna's direction.

'Fine, so you stay back and enjoy the party. I need to get going right away,' I said and stormed out of the bar, ignoring the couple of times I heard him call out my name. Poka, of course, did not follow me. His priorities were clear, they had always been.

I got down from the auto-rickshaw, paid the guy, and without waiting for the change went up to the flat. Battery was in the living room when I opened the door using my key. Ignoring his quizzical stare I headed straight to my room and dumped myself on the bed. Just like that, without even bothering to change.

A couple of hours later I was still sprawled on the bed, staring at the ceiling, when I heard the doorbell ring. Poka had not yet returned, so I assumed it was him. Perhaps he was too sloshed to attempt fitting his key into the lock, I thought, not bothering to twitch a muscle. I heard the main door open and soon after I heard a knock on the door to my room.

Poka wouldn't go about knocking the door even if he was suffering from amnesia, I knew. 'Who is it?' I asked, pulling myself up on my elbows.

'It's me,' I heard Battery's voice, followed by the door coming slightly ajar and his head emerging from the crack. Now the knock did make some sense. It was Battery being his natural self. 'What is it?' I nearly screamed. He was the last person I wanted to enter into a conversation with at that hour.

'Shalini is here. She wants to see you, she says. I came to check if I could send her inside. I mean…,' he whispered. I knew perfectly well what he meant. Poka's bad habit of sleeping in his boxers had rubbed on to me and Battery only wanted to make sure that I was in a state presentable enough to permit a girl to walk into the room. I nodded.

'Why did you leave without even saying a goodbye?' she grumbled as soon as she entered the room. She had a put-on frown on her face, one that usually did things to my heart, but not now. The frown was completely ineffective in wake of the fury bottled within me.

'Oh, so you noticed? I thought you were too preoccupied to be bothered,' I retorted in a tone dripping with scorn.

I was half-expecting her to snub me, cut me down to size, but the reaction she gave left me amazed. She smiled at me, one of her endearing, affectionate smiles. Confused, I continued looking at her.

'Oh, so you were jealous? That's a sign… Mr. Singh, you know what, you are in love with me,' she eventually spoke, the smile still affixed to her face.

'What crap?' I returned. I was startled at being confronted with something I had not yet come to terms with myself. Was she trying to get away with the fact that she had been in the arms of another man by putting an allegation of being in love upon me? How very lame, I mused.

'Hey, it is my birthday today… and you are not supposed to talk to me like that,' she said, putting on the frown once again. I refrained from reacting.

'Shall we stop kidding ourselves Rahul?' she continued, suddenly sounding somewhat serious. 'You know, when I saw you talking to those girls at the bar, I felt bad. I don't know why, but

I did. I realised it was probably because I have become possessive about you at some level. It was a pang of jealousy. So, to check if I was the only one bitten by the bug or it had got to you as well, I decided to shake a leg with Varun. And look what it did to you Mr. Singh. Let's face it, we are in love. I love you and you love me.'

She had unflinchingly said all that she wanted to, with a smile even, but I was shivering just trying to comprehend the implications of her words. I was still dumbfounded when she stepped forward to embrace me. It was tight, warm and lasted for a long time. I am sure neither of us wanted to let go, but our positions – I half-raised from the bed and she bending to meet me midway – were extremely uncomfortable and there was only as much ache in the limbs that our newfound love could help us endure.

As soon as the embrace ended, I jumped out of the bed and reached out for her once again. Our lips met, and I felt I was instantly transported to a different world. The experience was divine. It wasn't my first kiss and I had a feeling it wasn't hers either, but it was 'our' first kiss and that made the occasion momentous. My heart was beating so furiously that I could almost hear it. And then it coughed - my heart.

I was still trying to figure what her touch had done to get my heart coughing when abruptly she stepped back and looked towards the door. Poka stood there, looking at us with a mischievous grin and a rascally glint in his eyes. His fist moved up to his lips as he coughed once again.

Four

If love were a warrior, it would be a champion of the art of clandestine warfare. It strikes its preys when they are least suspecting, like a cat in stealthy pursuit, leaving no opportunity for them to forge an escape. It was some time before I realised that I too had been claimed by it, the latest among the countless victims of love.

The experience following Shalini's candid admission was like that of being caught in a quicksand pit – I could wiggle and squirm all that I wanted, but the rapid sinking was inevitable. The only difference, and a significant one at that, was that I was relishing every bit of the experience. I was drowning myself in love and loving every moment of it.

Shalini and I had started creating a small world of our own, a secluded existence within the larger space we physically inhibited, that we liked to escape into every once in a while. This private world of ours was nothing short of a wonderland for me. It was here that I discovered a side to Shalini which had remained hidden from me all this while and perhaps also from others who had ever known her.

Beneath her façade of boldness and aplomb hid an innocent and frail little girl with a strong need to be loved and to be pampered. She was sensitive and caring, not only towards me but towards everything that surrounded her. It was only that she hated to expose this side of hers to the world, the vulnerable side, as she often referred to it.

Only when we were together, just the two of us, that she opened up sometimes, allowing me a glimpse of her delicate interiors. When we watched a movie, she would feel for the protagonist and lament the wrongs inflicted upon him or her by the on-screen bad guys. If she saw someone pelting a stone at a stray dog, she would not intervene, but she would curse under her breath and feel sorry for the mongrel. And yet, on every other occasion she was still the strong, self-sufficient Shalini that I had admired when we first met.

We had our tiffs too, just like every other couple bound by the ties of love, but never anything drastic or long-lasting. It was simple, both of us could not stay without each other for long, and when we did fight, it was only a matter of time that one of us walked up to the other and apologised (irrespective of where the responsibility of starting the quarrel rested), pacifying the situation almost instantly.

'Don't you get it? This is not a freaking homeless shelter where each one in the queue will be served food. It is a job we are talking about for God's sake… and if the economic indicators are anything to go by, half our batch is going to remain unplaced,' I voiced my frustrations.

We were in Shalini's flat, in her room, and were sharing a joint after a passionate session of love-making. As is usually the case, once the testosterone surge had abruptly abated, I was left staring at the most abject realities confronting my life. The most compelling one, of course, was the need to graduate with a well-paying job in hand.

For nearly two years now I had managed to shut my eyes to the inevitable. I had so engrossed myself in living life to its hilt and seeking pleasures from its little bestowals that I had remained oblivious to the larger purpose which had got me to Mumbai in the first place. And now, when the placement week was barely a month away, I could feel pangs of anxiety gripping me at an alarming regularity. It wasn't just me; all others in my class had undergone a drastic change over the past couple of weeks too – since the day the final semester examination schedule had been put up, to be precise.

The brash and loud ones had suddenly turned quiet and brooding, while those known to be jovial and cheerful could be seen strolling purposelessly with their jaws nearly touching their chests. Reality had dawned en masse leaving an entire crop of young minds reeling under nervousness and severe performance pressure. This was the climax, the culmination of two crucial years of our young lives, and it was this – the job we could walk out with – that would determine the course of our remaining years.

Matters were made worse by the fact that in our kind of B-Schools (read B-listed) the Zero Day (supposedly the first day of placements when the coveted employers got their pick of the best talents on offer) lasted for weeks and sometimes even months. Any company consenting to visit the campus and offering a reasonable salary package was welcomed with open arms and any day its officials choose to conduct the interviews became yet another de facto Zero Day. This year, the prevailing economic scenario, reeling under the slowdown of the major western markets, was further threatening to torment us and stories of companies declining requests to visit the institute for recruitment were reaching our ears on an everyday basis.

I was scared and had voiced my concerns to Shalini.

Her chosen field of education did not warrant her to be an expert on matters concerning B-School placements and she ended up saying only what she was equipped to – a lecture of sorts on how I needed to remain positive and things would work out on their own.

I was irritated. Not only because of her ill-informed ranting, but also because I knew that Shalini would never understand my situation. She came from a family where they could afford to feed their cattle (if they ever decided to rear any) a seven-course meal three times a day.

Her father was a political bigwig, a name that flashed regularly in the 'City' pages of Delhi newspapers and was sometimes seen on one or the other television news channel too. I knew that she would never have to worry about commonplace things like placements and career, and that made me mad. Perhaps it was a form of jealousy, some warped and unreasonable form, which was getting the better of me.

'I understand the cause for your irritation, but tell me, is this going to help you in any manner, or improve your situation from where it stands? The situation demands that you give your best to any and every opportunity that comes up… and for that you need to be happy, smiling…' Allowing the words to tail, she leaned forward and capped my lips with her own. I was in half-a-mind to shove her away, but that would have been disastrous. Moreover, at that moment she was clad only in her black, netted negligee, a sight that could make the best among men lose their focus. So I complied, albeit passively. The lip-lock didn't last long and pulling back abruptly she said, 'I think it is about time I spoke to my father.'

'What? Are you out of your mind? Here is me, worried like man on death row, and all you can think of is telling your parents about us? Couldn't you at least wait for a better time to bring this up?'

'Not us, silly! I intend to speak with him about your job. I will tell my father that you are a close friend and that he should help you. I am sure he will figure out something,' she said.

Her words were reassuring. Some misplaced sense of pride was pricking me to ask her to keep her family out of my problems, but I was quick to quash it. Ends justify the means, I told myself. Moreover, I wasn't aware of Shalini's background when we started dating, so no one could accuse me of being a wily no-gooder, an opportunist who had latched on to her for reasons other than merely love. It was purely an act of fate that she happened to be from such a family and I was no fool to abstain from the perks which were nothing but a natural consequence.

True to her word, the very next day Shalini handed me a piece of paper with an e-mail id scribbled on it, instructing me to mail across my resume and mention her father's name as a reference. One look at the id and my soaring hopes came crashing down like a house of cards. Embedded in the id was the name of one of the most prestigious consultancy firms in the country, a firm which limited its recruitment to the top three management schools of the country. Campuses like ours didn't even bother with inviting them for placements. This was a lead that wasn't ever going to fructify. They were not going to touch a guy with academic credentials like mine with a ten foot pole.

However, just because Shalini had made the effort to speak to her father, I did as she suggested, certain that I wasn't even going to get an acknowledgement for my e-mail. But I was wrong. The very next day I received a call from a heavily accented lady who introduced herself as an HR (Human Resources) Manager from the same firm. She fixed up an interview for me with one of the firm partners at their Mumbai office and the rest is history. Not only was I one of the first people from my batch to get placed, but my package and the company I was to join was certain to feature in the institute prospectus for years to come.

It was later I learnt that my employers were engaged in rendering high value consultancy services to the government and it was through a friend of Shalini's father that their assignments got routed. That put a lot of things in perspective. Also, while surfing the Internet in preparing for my interview, I stumbled across a familiar name, Mr. Sinha, the India Managing Director of the firm. It was the man I had e-mailed my resume to.

We celebrated my entry into the corporate world in style. Using the last penny in my bank account, I booked a weekend package in one of the city five-star hotels (The initial plan was for a weekend jaunt to Goa, but I was yet to draw my first pay-check and until that happened Goa was anything but affordable), all with a spa booking in the couples' room, meals in their exotic restaurants and access to the discothèque and other luxuries the property boasted of. It was a surprise for Shalini, and to keep it so, I had to resort to some degree of sleight.

I landed up at her flat on Saturday morning and, waking her from sleep, asked her to get ready at once. I told her that I had got tickets for a movie which had released just the previous day. Since it was a highly anticipated film, I couldn't get tickets for any of the evening shows, I reasoned, to further substantiate my claim. She took the bait and rushed into the bathroom. Taking advantage of the situation, I scanned her wardrobe and shoved the items I thought were necessary into the small bag I was carrying. If the bag's presence or that there was a taxi waiting for us when we stepped out of the apartment gate, aroused any suspicions in her mind, she did well to contain them. She seemed genuinely surprised, somewhat confused even, when the taxi dropped us at the hotel porch.

Those two days would easily rate among the best times that Shalini and I have ever spent together. We did all that we had ever dreamt of doing – playing out our passionate kinks, frolicking uninhibitedly in the swimming pool and holding hands and staring into each other's eyes over a candle-lit dinner – making it into a honeymoon of sorts. And rightfully so, for that is how I had introduced ourselves – a newlywed couple looking for some much needed respite from a household infested with relatives – to the hotel's booking executive I had spoken to while making the reservation.

The spa session turned out to be a particularly memorable one. The preliminary reticence from lying on adjoining beds clad in flimsy nothings with strange hands kneading our bodies, to eventually finding comfort, adjusting with the unfamiliar but exhilarating nature of the surroundings, was an ethereal experience. Nothing like anything I had ever experienced in the past. By the time the two masseuses (we had opted for both female hands) were wrapping up, we were both so aroused that as soon as they left the room, leaving us to shower and change, we very nearly jumped upon each other. The celebration had cost me my life's savings, but it was well worth the money. Moreover, it was only a matter of time that money, with its promise of abundance, would cease to remain such a crucial consideration for me.

My inhibitions in working for a reputed consultancy firm and the complexities I had been nursing about my deficient aptitude were dispelled within the first few weeks of my joining work. The office was nothing but an assemblage of people, each unique and diverse in thoughts, actions and mannerisms, just like my campus had been. While the people in office appeared more serious and business-like, the moulds used for their fabrication weren't, in reality, very different from those that the folks back in my institute came from.

Once you managed to get beyond their stern exteriors, gave them the comfort they needed to open up, most of them were warm, friendly and fun people to be with. Since I had age by my side, the youngest kid on the block, it took me little time to find my footing. In the minds of my colleagues, I was the fresh energetic fellow who posed no threat to them. They were all forthcoming and amiable towards me and soon I found myself assigned to the team managing an extremely crucial project for the firm.

If it merits a mention, this was the same project that the firm had been engaged for by the government and by way of which Shalini's father had chanced upon a connection with its Managing Director.

It wouldn't be wrong if I said that the corporate world was being kind to me, unlike most other batchmates of mine who had horrific tales to tell of the start to their work lives. I was being made to work and justify my salary of course, but not without a senior member of the project team guiding me at each stage.

My mistakes, the few that I committed, were looked upon as 'opportunities for improvement' rather than 'errors' and I can't remember being reprimanded for any. Though initially my job was limited to data crunching, analysis and preparing PowerPoint slides, I was enjoying every bit of it, especially the immense learning potential it presented. So, for five days of the week I would immerse myself in my work, trying to give my best to every little task that landed on my desk, and during the weekends I would devote myself to Shalini.

Our lives, Shalini's and mine, were by now entwined to an extent that we couldn't imagine staying without each other. Fuddu had got a job in Kolkata while Poka had been picked up for a marketing role with an IT firm in Bangalore (he claimed that they were planning a foray into pornographic portals and thus the obvious choice of candidate) and both had moved to their respective destinations since.

Battery had joined a Mumbai-based bank and he and I shared our flat now. We had mutually decided against getting new roommates to replace the two who had left as it allowed us the comfort to keep a bedroom each. Not to mention that with our newfound statuses of salaried professionals, we could afford splitting the rent two ways.

The girls too remained in the same flat - all three of them - even after Shalini and Ishita completed their graduation. While Ishita had started working as a merchandiser with an export house, Shalini had opted to assist an established fashion designer and further hone her skills along the way. Shalini's job didn't pay much but money had never been a consideration for her. In fact I even had my doubts whether she was as passionate about fashion designing as she sometimes claimed. But her job allowed us to remain together and beyond that nothing else seemed to matter.

At work, it took me little time to graduate from being a mere back-end support for the team to becoming an integral part of it. Soon I found myself being involved in client meetings and visits, an evolution that had me travelling to several government offices around the country. I didn't mind the travel but it meant that when in town, I had to devote enough time to Shalini so as to maintain the balance.

I made it a point to pick Shalini from her workplace whenever I could and we would go out, savouring the scrumptious delicacies sold on the streets of Mumbai or eating at a plush fine-dine restaurant, driving aimlessly sometimes and visiting our favourite sea-facing coffee shop when we felt like. At night, it was usually my room that we stayed in. I still hadn't found my comfort zone with Prerna while Battery remained non-interfering as always, making the choice fairly obvious. It was as if we were in a live-in relationship without actually using the living-in tag.

Our weekends were especially crazy and now that we could afford the pleasures we wished, we found ourselves at one or the other swanky joint every Saturday, partying till the wee hours. Shalini's work brought her in contact with several interesting people, unlike the boring consultants I was surrounded with, and this was the group of people we preferred to hang out with – models (mostly aspiring ones, severely burdened by misconceptions about their looks), designers and other fancy characters that could bring life to the dullest of gatherings. I, thanks to my line of work, found myself being regarded with reverence by most among the bunch – a fact that I quietly cherished and I suspected Shalini did too.

'Rohit is throwing a party tomorrow to announce his fall winter collection. It will be a grand affair, a Page 3 party. We are invited too,' Shalini announced one Friday evening. The excitement in her tone was palpable. Till then I had met most of her colleagues from work, but for Rohit, her boss. However, through Shalini and the others, I had heard so much about him that, and of course the entertainment channels on television where he was a regular feature, he no longer seemed like a stranger. The party sounded interesting going by the manner Shalini had described it and I had no reasons to turn down the invite.

The next evening at the appointed hour we were at the ballroom of a prestigious suburban hotel, the venue for Rohit's party. Shalini was wearing a black Lycra dress that ended just where her thighs began. It was a full-sleeved garment with a deep neckline and an even deeper cut at the back. It not only gave Shalini the illusion of being taller than she actually was (or perhaps that credit went to her heels), but also made her look smoking hot. I could sense curious eyes surveying her as we made our way through the hotel lobby towards the ballroom and I felt my chest bloat with pride.

Her attire was such that had she walked out of our apartment complex dressed like that, she would certainly have caused a series of heart attacks. I shudder to even think about the effect she would have had on the indolent guard usually found manning the society gates in the late evening hours – the poor fellow probably would have had to submerge himself in a tank full of holy water from the river Ganges to recover from the shock. Thankfully Shalini had used an old gown for temporary cover which she shed in my car within moments of leaving the complex.

'Oh my God… You look gorgeous darling… And this must be your boyfriend. A handsome catch, I must say.' Rohit was there at the gate personally receiving his guests, and I got a first-hand demonstration of the theatrics I had seen him engage in during his television appearances. He was highly animated, twitching his brows and blinking his eyes with every word he spoke. He held my hand for just that wee bit longer, an unnerving experience given that his preference for men wasn't really a closely guarded secret.

The hall wasn't particularly large, just the right size to take in about two hundred guests. On the two furthest corners were bar counters, partly concealed by the patrons waiting to grab their glasses. The party was just about beginning and the crowd already appeared in excess of fifty, some familiar faces - Shalini's colleagues - peppering the unfamiliar ones. There were models posing in random but well-lit sections of the room in what appeared to be garments from Rohit's new collection – clothes that did more to reveal their size-zero bodies than conceal them – and a bunch of photographers were crowding them for a good click.

The party, I learnt, was a precursor of sorts for some of the premium fashion magazines and Rohit's principal buyers. It was strictly a business affair. A party meant to create the desired buzz before the line was introduced to the general public. If this was business, I asked myself, what do they do when they feel like having fun? Looking at the guests drowning in expensive alcohol and legitimately eyeing half-nude beauties, I couldn't help but ponder if I had made the correct career choice. I would have fared significantly better in such a surrounding, undoubtedly.

'You see that man… the fat one… there… He is Mr. Chowksi,' Shalini whispered, signalling from the corner of her eye towards an ostentatiously dressed and large man with enough gold on him to put Fort Knox to shame.

'He is one of the most renowned garment exporters in the country. Rohit expects him to confirm a large order today so he has already reserved the presidential suite of the hotel for him. If Mr. Chowksi does what is expected of him, he will be spending his night there with a couple of these models.' As she winked to drive home her point, my eyes nearly fell off their sockets. No, I hadn't turned into some self-appointed moral custodian for the fashion industry, but the thought of Mr. Chowksi atop any of those frail-looking girls was simply unconceivable. He would have quashed them to pulp. I would have found it easier to imagine him mounting an elephant, with some bit of sympathy reserved for the animal of course.

Even as I was struggling to erase the absurd images that her words had created in my mind, Shalini patted my hand and said, 'I will be right back.' I saw her cut through a couple of groups before disappearing into the crowd. The party was in full swing now with people nearly spilling out of the banquet hall.

I had realised by now that for those who worked with Rohit, Shalini included, the party was nothing but a networking forum. They were expected to engage with the invitees, buyers especially, and look for any opportunity that could translate into business. Shalini had been leaving me every now and then, sometimes in the company of her colleagues and sometimes alone, like now, to go about her duties. I wasn't peeved to the slightest bit as the party had enough on offer to keep me from getting bored.

There were girls, prettier than any I had set my eyes on, wandering about in dresses that made Shalini look like a thoroughly wrapped up mummy. In Shalini's presence I couldn't be seen drooling, so I was eyeing them as inconspicuously as I could manage. I was engaged in escorting a pair of firm, hot pants-clad buttocks to the bar counter, with my eyes of course, when I felt a palm graze my shoulder.

'Hey handsome,' a near whisper reached my ears. I turned to face Rohit who was brazenly flashing his dentures, swaying peculiarly as he did so. I returned a genial smile.

'I see that your sweetheart has left you unattended. She should be more careful with something as delightful and delicious as you. Rahul… wasn't that your name? Oh, how masculine that sounds,' he continued, grabbing my hand in the garb of a second introduction.

'Thanks,' I managed to mutter, struggling to retain my fast

fading smile. The man (or whatever he was), his words, the manner in which he was holding my hand, it was all very unsettling. I hate to admit, but I was feeling threatened, violated nearly. I wanted to pull my hand out of his grip, use it to sock him where it would hurt the most and walk out of there, but he was our host. Moreover he was Shalini's boss. I had to remain cordial.

'You are a consultant I hear. Now isn't that a waste of such a fabulous body?' he said, taking a step forward and using his other hand to run a circle on my chest. He was now so close to me that his perfume, a strong feminine fragrance, was piercing through my nostrils. Then, with a slight movement of the hand he was using to clutch mine, he brushed my hands across his crotch and winked. 'You should try your hand at modelling. I could do something for you, you know,' he added.

'Rohit, Rahul is happy being a consultant. Let's just leave him where he is, shall we?' It was Shalini. Like a knight in shining armour she had appeared out of nowhere to save me from the clutches of evil, literally. She was smiling as she addressed her boss, but the finality in her tone was apparent. Rohit let go of my hand at once, staring at Shalini with the look of a dog which had just been robbed of its bone.

'My, my, are we getting possessive or what? But darling you know what; sometimes it works best to share the good things we possess. For all you know he might be walking the ramp for your own clothes line, the one you have always wanted to design. Moreover, what is the problem if he does to me what he has been doing to you all this while? It will only hone his skills,' he replied wickedly.

'Enough,' she said. She was gritting her teeth and her eyes had suddenly turned amber. She wasn't loud, but her voice was cold as ice and could slice through a slab of wood with ease. I was furious too, at the way her slimy boss was trying to strike a bargain for dragging me to his bed. I felt like a prostitute and suddenly my respect for those engaged in the oldest known profession shot up a notch. But even before my reactions could find a vent, Shalini had started speaking once again.

'You sick son of a bitch! You think the lure of designing my own line or a chance to walk the ramp is such a big deal that you can get us to do anything you like? Let me be the one to dispel your notions then, you can go and shove the line up where you will pleasure from it the most. I care two hoots about you, your fucking job and this party… got it? You are standing straight only because I don't want the newspapers to be splashed with images of you getting thrashed; else I would have shown you how much of a wimp you really are. I am going right now, but this is not the last you have seen of me. I will be there in office on Monday and if the cheque settling all my dues is not ready by then, you can brace yourself for a hell-of-a time,' she said, before storming out of the party. I was close on her heels.

She kept cursing Rohit for half our drive back and then suddenly she looked into my eyes and said, 'Rahul, you know what, let's just get married.'

'What?' I nearly sprang from my seat. I couldn't look back at her, control the steering and restrain my rapidly thumping heart, all at once, so I swerved the vehicle to the side and brought it to a screeching halt. Thankfully it was late in the night and there wasn't much traffic on the road, else, who knows what I would have banged into. I was anyways bumping into strange things today.

'What did you say?' I asked, turning to lock her gaze as soon as the car stopped.

'You heard me,' she said. 'Let us get married.'

She had a strange twinkle in her eyes and was sporting the same mischievous grin that made the world around me fade into oblivion. I leaned to the left and, ignoring the gearstick which was poking me in strange places, reached out for her. She shifted slightly and we were soon embracing, my face buried at the side of her neck, taking in the scent that was uniquely hers. Gradually my lips crawled towards hers and we exploded in a wild frenzy as soon as they met. We had just sealed our fate in the only manner we knew how to do so.

Five

It wasn't immediate; we took some time, about three months or so, before our impending marriage was formalised. Shalini, post quitting her job, had announced that since it was only a matter of time before we got married, she would take a break from work and resume only after the wedding. She, or rather, her father, was abundantly capable of funding her unwaged stay in Mumbai, so who was I to complain?

For her it was the task of convincing her parents for the marriage that proved challenging, but in the end she succeeded. No sooner had she expressed her desire to get married to me, telephonically of course, she was barraged with the standard set of questions aimed at steering her towards reasonableness – What does the boy do? How much does he earn? What is the family like? How much property do they own? What is their dog's blood-group? How many bones does he chew in a day? And so on and so forth.

But the same haughty, obstinate blood ran in her veins too and she knew exactly how to get her way with them. It took her a couple of trips back home, some melodramatic sulking and an unwavering resolve, but they were soon towing her line. The two families met to discuss the way forward, her folks sitting like they had been made to do so at gunpoint and mine with a sense of awe as if they were visiting the White House to seek the President's daughter's hand in marriage.

Shalini, meanwhile, had ensured that the list of possible outcomes from the meeting was restricted to one – the one she had bullyingly pushed down her father's throat – and we were not surprised when the deliberations concluded with an agreement on the month of our marriage. It was the coming November. The auspicious date was left for the pundits to arrive upon, but we had five months, give or take a few weeks, before we would be exchanging the wedding vows.

Within a month of our marriage being finalised, I was summoned by one of the firm partners into his cabin. Smiling, he handed me a sealed envelope, his gaze affixed on me while I opened it, as if he were expecting a bunch of pigeons to flutter out of the packet. The packet contained a folded letter and the first word I saw as I unfolded it was, 'Congratulations'. I had been promoted as a Senior Associate and my already substantial pay packet had turned heftier. I left the cabin beaming, restraining myself from screaming out aloud. This was simply fantastic.

I had completed two years with the firm and it wasn't unheard of for people to get promoted in that sort of a timespan. I had been faring well, by my own modest judgment, on the tasks I was now handling. However, as much as I wished to attribute the break to my own hard work or even a stroke of good fortune, somewhere deep in my heart I knew that there was more to it than met the eye. But what the hell! I was a pragmatic man and as long as the happenings were in line with my wants, there was no reason to complain.

Shalini had buried herself neck-deep in 'marriage preparations', as she liked to call her present engagement. For me it was a lot of wasteful expenditure, but I was aware of her proclivity for shopping and thus, in my own better interest, I refrained from voicing my opinions. Meekly, I went about accompanying her during the shopping sprees, designer appointments and fitting sessions. A practice for the times to come, I told myself.

She appeared intent on re-attiring half the populace of Delhi, picking up random garments for aunts I had never heard of and cousins I didn't know existed and in the bargain claiming nearly every minute of the time I could manage outside of office.

However, the unexpected increment had sprouted a thought in my mind which, after much deliberation, had mushroomed into an agenda of my own. Stealthily I embarked upon exploration and research which the project demanded. Shalini could have helped but given her preoccupations, I decided to bring her on it only when the time was right. I wanted to buy a house. A dream for every individual who comes to the city in pursuit of a career, and one that I could now afford to realise. My increased salary could either go in funding Shalini's ceaseless shopping or in paying EMIs (Equated Monthly Instalments) for a house we could call our own. The choice was amply clear, at least as far as I was concerned.

It took a couple of months and I managed to find a two-bedroom flat in Juhu, a premium residential locality not far from the area we were currently residing in, that came within my reach after a minor stretch in the initially planned budget. It was a surprise for Shalini and I had to nearly abduct her to take her to see the flat. She was full of questions and comments – Where are we going? Why? There is so much left to be done. Why can't we leave whatever you have on your mind for another day and go to the jeweller instead?

But once she saw the flat, she was ecstatic. She was so happy that I felt a surge of guilt at not having involved her in the search process earlier.

Armed with her concurrence, I engaged myself in the paperwork – the loan application, sale agreement, registration of the property etc. – while Shalini returned to her shopping with a renewed vigour. She had suddenly found another goal to be pursued: The beautification of our new house. Even before the flat's possession had been formally handed over to us, she had collected enough paraphernalia to do it up twice over. Every little knick knack she picked, she would exhibit before me like a child displaying her first ever painting, and I would smile, deriving my pleasures from her little ones.

Meanwhile, it had been agreed between both sets of parents that the wedding would take place in Delhi. When Shalini said that her folks were planning a 'small affair' I believed her, because I wasn't exactly a prized catch for a groom from where they came. Her father's inhibition in parading me – a man for whom his salary was the only means of livelihood – before his peers and colleagues was perfectly valid. It also meant that my parents, who had agreed to travel to Delhi with a small contingent of relatives for the ceremony, would not be as intimidated as I had initially feared.

But I should have known better. Shalini's family was still following a definition of the word 'small' that probably dated back to the age of the dinosaurs. The setting for the marriage left us flummoxed. It was a farmhouse on the outskirts of the city, a palace-like place, lit-up and decorated in the manner that the city of Ayodhya must have been for Lord Ram's homecoming. It was a single event, a reception-cum-dinner at the same venue followed by the marriage ceremony sometime late into the night. As I sat on the dais, waiting for Shalini to surface, I began counting the attendees to keep myself occupied. It was after five hundred that I gave up and I hadn't even covered half the faces that I could see ahead of me.

The marriage went off smoothly. Well at least most of it. Shalini's parents, despite their initial reluctance to the communion, had managed to keep their energy levels soaring, introducing me to countless relatives and friends with enthusiasm that made me feel like I was the groom they had always dreamt of for their daughter. My little contingent, thirty two in all, including close family and friends, had been swallowed by the crowd like needles in a haystack. Barring my parents and a couple of close friends who kept coming up to the makeshift stage every once in a while, I couldn't even trace the others for most part of the evening.

Yes, now to the slight glitch. It wasn't anything major, just a little mix-up involving, well, guess who?

Poka!

Poka had travelled from Bangalore to attend the wedding. I was meeting him after long and yet I could figure that the fabled Bangalore weather had done little to change him. In fact, if anything, he only seemed more eager and excited than I had ever known him to be – a bull on a rampage after having snapped its tether.

'Man, look at these Delhi babes… they are so… so… huge,' he had said, rolling his eyes in disbelief and moving his neck sideways to cover the entire gamut of womankind in the range of his vision. We were in the lobby of the hotel where the girl's side had arranged for our lodging.

While my family and I had arrived the previous day, two days prior to the marriage, most of my friends had only begun trickling in today. When Poka called me from the lobby I rushed down to meet him. It was with Poka that I had seen some of the wildest times of my life and I was keen to catch up with him after a gap of two long years.

'You will never change, will you? A hello wouldn't have been bad to start with, though,' I said teasingly, reaching out to hug him. Once we were done with our customary embrace, he eyed me from head to toe, his hands resting on my shoulders. 'Wow, I can't believe this. You guys are actually getting married, you and Shalini… Isn't that amazing?' he said, bursting into a chuckle as if he had just cracked a funny joke. I kept smiling, looking at him and wondering how little he had changed over the past two years.

'Dude, so where is the party tonight?' he asked once he had managed to gather his breath.

'There is no party tonight. We will all retire early so that we are up in time for the rituals scheduled for tomorrow morning. You can party all that you want at the reception tomorrow.'

'Bull shit! Your marriage and we don't have a bachelors' party... now, that I will not allow. Not over my dead body. Have Fuddu and Battery arrived already?'

I nodded my head.

'Don't worry, now that I am here, I will take care of everything,' he said with a wink. 'Just put me up with either one of those guys or in a separate single room. We will need all the privacy we can manage.'

'Are you crazy? My parents are here; my entire family is here... Forget about a bachelors' party, I can't even drink tonight, not even a beer. Yes, you guys can have all that you want and put the tab on the room. That will be taken care of.'

'Oh, so now you think we can't even pay for our booze...,' he retorted, looking hurt.

'No, that's not what I meant...'

'Chill dude,' he said, cutting me short and breaking into another spell of laughter. 'I was only pulling your leg. I know what you mean and what you don't. Likewise you should know that when I mean something, I really mean it. So, stop being a sissy and just land up where I tell you to.'

I tried to reason with him, fully conscious about the futility of my efforts, and Poka, as expected, remained beyond the realms of reason and rationality. So, to make the affair as discrete as possible, I requested the reception clerk to check Poka into a single room on a floor different from the other guests.

A party arranged by Poka was very likely to turn wild at some point, and it was best that my parents be kept away from it lest they found compelling reasons to disown me on the eve of my marriage. Or worse, for some of my elderly relatives, the party, if held in their proximity, had the potential of turning fatal too. For, who knew what shocks their ageing hearts might end up having to endure?

I arrived in Poka's room at the appointed hour, giving my mother some spiel about friends insisting on my company over dinner, intending to keep away from alcohol. While Poka, Battery and Fuddu were there, I was surprised to find two other friends, my college mates from Pune who the other three had no means of being acquainted with, happily sitting inside and sipping their drinks.

'Rascals have a way of befriending other rascals. We can smell our own kind in a crowd,' sensing my curiosity, Poka explained. The five burst out guffawing instantly, and I joined them.

It began with one drink – a gesture to strengthen the bonds of our friendship, I was told – and it never ended. We sat there, doing what a bunch of boys usually do when drinking, sharing stories – mostly boisterous tales of having made out with some or the other girl – and laughing at inane things. It was nice, a welcome respite of carefree carousal from the humdrum professional lives we had each embarked upon. I felt young again, like a teenager brimming with newfound lust for life.

I would have been on my fourth drink when the telephone in the room began to ring. I looked at the faces around, the clock on the bedside table, and then hurriedly picked up the receiver. It was a little after two in the night.

'Is that Mr. Rahul Singh?' I heard a deep-set voice on the line.

'Yes this is Rahul. Who is this?'

'Sir, I am calling from the hotel reception. Apologies for disturbing you at this hour, but we need your presence here urgently. Would it be possible for you to come down to the lobby please?' The expressions on my face would have changed, for all the four guys were curiously staring at me now.

'Why? What happened?' I shot back.

'Sir, I can't explain it to you over the phone. It is extremely important that you come down right away. Had it not been an urgent matter, I would not have disturbed you so late in the night.'

Putting the phone down, I looked at the others, my heart beating profusely. It was then that I realised that one of them was missing, Poka. About 15 minutes back, or maybe 20, his mobile phone had rung, and clutching it, he had slipped out the door. In our merry-making the rest of us had failed to notice that he hadn't yet returned. Suddenly I was nearly hysterical with randomly darting thoughts. 'It must be Poka. He must have done something,' I murmured after I had summarised my conversation with the receptionist for the benefit of others.

I asked Battery to accompany me and leaving the others to wait for us in the room, headed towards the lift. As the lift paced down to the lobby, a drop of ten floors in just a few seconds, I felt a tingling sensation in my ears, like a gush of air was passing right through my head. It must be the drinks, I thought. I hadn't had one in days. Steadying myself, I stepped out into a near desolate lobby. Not surprising given the time of the night.

'Which way?' Battery whispered in my ears and I felt like socking him in the face.

Without uttering a word, I dashed to the reception. There was no one behind the desk but I could see human forms through an open door not far from the counter. Then, perhaps having heard our approaching steps, someone stepped out of the door – a man clad in a black jacket and a matching necktie, the standard uniform for receptionists at the hotel.

'Mr. Singh?' he asked me. He was the same man who had called me in the room. I nodded. 'Would you mind stepping in here for a minute?' he said, extending his hand towards the open door.

I complied, only to step into a scene so strange that it surpassed my wildest imaginings.

The room was small, eight by eight feet at most. On a chair resting against one of the side walls was Poka, looking furious, and two menacing looking men in safari suits were standing on his sides, almost flanking him. Members of the hotel security staff, I gathered. Another man, the assistant manager whom I had briefly interacted with for room allocation of my guests was seated behind a wooden desk on the only other chair in the room. Two women, or maybe girls, clad in untidy looking salwar suits and wearing bright red lipsticks stood fidgeting behind Poka's chair.

'Hey, Rahul…' Poka said, emerging from the chair and feigning a sheepish smile.

'Sir, please allow me to have a word with him first,' the assistant manager cut through Poka's greeting before turning to look at me. His voice instantly slipped a couple of decibels as he addressed me. 'Sir, please accept my apologies for disturbing you, but the gentleman here was trying to take these girls inside the hotel. We are a reputed establishment, you know, and we do not encourage any such activities that might come in the way of our reputation or discomfit our elite clientele.

One of our guards intercepted them to check who the ladies were and the gentleman here lost his cool. He began screaming at the guard, accusing him of ill-treating hotel guests. It was with much difficulty and upon my intervention that we were able to pacify him and get him here. Thankfully we don't have very many customers in the lobby at this hour else the scene he created might have compelled us to evict him that very instant.

Anyway, now he claims that the ladies are your friends and that you have invited them here for your party,' he paused briefly to glance at Poka. 'So, we thought we should bring the incident to your notice and also confirm if the girls are indeed your friends.'

I turned to look at the girls. As I did so, one of them, the one in the greenish dress of the kind of fabric they once used to make car seat covers, looked at me and smiled.

'Hello,' she said, in a funny and confusing accent, a hybrid of several South and East Indian tongues. Coming from her, the Hello sounded like Yellow. And ironic as it was, there was another thing yellow that exposed itself when she spoke – the shade of her teeth, eventually merging into brown deposits around her gums. She was atrocious. Her companion, if I may draw comparisons, was only worse.

'No, I don't know them,' I said, avoiding Poka's restless glare entirely.

'Sir, you may enter the hotel if you so wish, but the ladies will not be permitted inside,' the manager decreed, addressing Poka. He had a redressed and satisfied look on his face. I turned on my heels and began walking towards the elevator.

'Wait up,' I heard Poka call out to me. When I didn't make any efforts to turn around or pause, he ran a few steps to catch up with me.

'What's with you, dude? Why couldn't you just say that you knew those girls?' he shot out as soon as he was alongside me. Standard Poka tactics, offence is the best form of defence. I could sense the tinge of embarrassment in his tone, but he was too uptight an individual to accept his mistakes openly. I chose to remain silent.

When his prodding did not stop, Battery had to intervene. 'Can we do this once we are back in the room instead of creating another scene here?' he said, sounding surprisingly assertive for the Battery of the past.

Once we had stepped inside the room and the door was shut behind us, all hell broke loose. The fury pent up within me gushed out in a torrent and I began showering Poka with all the invectives I could remember. How could he even attempt sneaking in prostitutes in the very hotel where my parents were lodged and the tab for which was being picked up by my in-laws to be? And what kind of girls were they anyway? Had he stooped to such low standards that anything that had an opening for him to 'poke' was fine with him?

Not one to be cowed down, Poka had found his own reasons to scream back. He accused me of having turned soft, of having abandoned a friend when I could have saved his face by simply acknowledging the girls. The ultimate was his assertion that he had done all this, taken all the pains, only because it was my bachelors' party and he wanted to make it a memorable one for me. 'Otherwise, I have no dearth of girls willing to sleep with me. I don't need to pay a prostitute to satisfy my sexual urges, not ever,' he added.

'Yeah, right! Did you even look at those girls? I wouldn't even wish to be seen dead with them, let alone take them to bed,' I screamed right back.

'But how was I to know what they would turn out like? The guy I spoke to over the phone said that they were extremely good-looking college students who did this for a hobby.'

'And what about when you saw them? Why did you still insist on getting them along with you?'

'What was I to do? I had already paid the guy in advance,' he reasoned. The explanation was so silly and preposterous that I burst out laughing. The others too saw the humour in the situation and began to laugh. Poka was the last to join in, and when he did, he was rolling on the floor clutching his stomach for a good ten minutes.

'But how on earth did you manage to find them? I mean, as far as I know, you have never been to Delhi before,' I enquired once order had been restored within the room.

'Don't you read newspapers? What do you think those 'decent masseuses at your doorstep' advertisements really are?' he quipped.

Once the matter was settled, it was time to cover our tracks. The repercussions could prove disastrous if my parents, or worse, Shalini's parents, were to learn about our adventures. Leaving the others to savour the remaining alcohol and Poka to continue his incessant bickering, I returned to the lobby. After doling out a hefty tip in exchange of a promise from the assistant manager that the happenings would not find their way to any undesired ears, I came back to my room and crashed for the night.

In a way it was good that Poka had been cut down to size ahead of the marriage ceremony for he was more than capable of leaving his mark on the most significant evening of my life too. So, with him putting up an unusually reticent façade, the reception and marriage went off as planned, with no unexpected appearances by strange girls or any other unforeseen hiccups.

Later, sometime in the wee hours of the morning, when we retired to our specially prepared room – Shalini and I, as Man and Wife – I was half expecting Poka to emerge from the closet with a camera in hand. To Shalini's utter dismay, I checked every nook that could serve as a hiding place for a full-grown man and only when I had convinced myself that Poka wasn't around that I made for the bed. Assured, I took off my Jodhpuri *jootis* and crawled onto the petal strewn bed where Shalini lay in wait.

Six

'Rise and shine Mr. Singh,' Shalini said, drawing apart the bedroom curtains. As the sun's rays bathed me, squinting, I pulled myself up and reached for the cup of tea she had placed at the bedside table. She was unusually chirpy today, and for good reason. In a day's time, our marriage was to turn two and we were heading to Goa to usher in our second anniversary. I smiled as I took a sip of the tea. It was terrible, too much sugar and too little milk. I should have made my own tea, as I usually did, but the gesture itself was moving and I had no option but to declare that it was a perfectly brewed cup of beverage.

Our marriage hadn't altered much as far as our relationship went. Yes, we were staying together legitimately now, but we were still the same Shalini and Rahul that we had always been. The few hours of vigorous chanting of sacred mantras by pundits who had charged a bomb to solemnise our marriage had done precious little to alter our inner selves. Therefore, once we returned from our honeymoon trip to Malaysia, it took little time for us to slip back in thrall of our respective lives.

The promotion, all the perks accompanying it aside, had also raised peoples' expectations from me and the quantum of work on my desk had suddenly increased manifold. I was spending a lot more time in the office now, returning well past dinner time on most days and sometimes working through weekends as well. And that, when I wasn't travelling.

Thankfully, Shalini's obsession with doing up our house had persisted over the next few months and she hadn't really taken badly to my continued absence. She had done well to transform the small apartment into a home, a truly stylish one at that. The drawing room was a combination of white, black and red with leather sofas, framed paintings and small artefacts that she had personally combed the markets for, adding to its exquisiteness. Our bedroom was done up in white, all of it, from the furniture to the upholstery, giving it a calm, serene look.

The transformation of the house, at least most of it, had happened without my participation or even cognizance. One Sunday, I would get up to realise that some part of the house looked different from when I had last noticed it. I would rattle my brains, trying to 'spot the difference' or simply turn to Shalini and allow her to animatedly share all that she had achieved over the past week. It was nice till it lasted, but once the interiors were done I was suddenly aware of all the free time Shalini had on her hands, leaving me with pangs of guilt at not being able to spend as much time with her as I would have liked.

She had not resumed work as against her original plans and in that I saw an answer to my quandary. I tried to talk to her about it, intending to convince her to start working once again, but each time she was quick to dismiss the subject altogether. It appeared as if fashion designing, an occupation she was once so passionate about, had lost its charm for her suddenly.

'What is it? Aren't you earning enough to manage our expenses that you are so belligerent about getting me back to work?' she had retorted once when I was trying to push the matter slightly. That was the last discussion we had regarding her career.

Shalini never complained about my demanding work schedule or the frequent travels that kept me away from her. This should have helped allay my guilt, but it did not. It wasn't that she empathised with my situation or even understood it. She had simply slipped into a habit of carrying on with life in my absence and that to me was disturbing. I felt bad each time I was packing my bags to embark upon an official trip and I felt worse when I saw that Shalini remained completely unperturbed by my impending departure.

Maybe I was wrong when I said that marriage hadn't changed us. It hadn't changed Shalini for sure. She remained the bubbly, carefree girl that she had been, caring about little and worrying about even lesser. Her friends from her erstwhile workplace and college still remained an integral part of her life and every second day she had a party or a get-together to attend with one group or the other. I was invited too, but it was seldom that I managed to accompany her.

But marriage had changed me perhaps. My expectations from Shalini, my wife, had gradually drifted away from the expectations I once had from Shalini, my girlfriend.

When I would return home to find Shalini passed out on the bed, her breath reeking of alcohol or the air laden with heady smell of marijuana, I couldn't help but feel frustrated. As I served my food, on days that the cook hadn't fallen sick and Shalini had remembered to leave some for me, else relying on the ever-so-dependable pack of instant noodles, I would be consumed by a feeling of hatred towards Shalini's lifestyle - the same way of life that had once drawn me to her.

It was only a matter of time that my frustrations began to show as cracks in our relationship. We were hardly spending any time together, each one buried neck-deep in the world of their choosing, and that had taken away the spark from our relationship. It took us the slightest of issues to start quarrelling. And when we did fight, neither of us would make an attempt at truce, preferring to let time play its part as the conciliator.

So much so that we had spent our last anniversary sulking confined in separate rooms of our flat. It was simply an insignificant issue blown out of proportion by our reducing tolerance for each other.

Since it was our first anniversary, my intention was to make it a memorable one for us both. I had booked a dinner table at one of the swankiest restaurants in town and picked up a pair of earrings as her gift. As soon as I reached home, I asked Shalini to get ready. She was excited too, perhaps sensing that I had a surprise in store. As she was going towards the bathroom, I called out to her and handed her the small packet making it seem like an afterthought. 'Why don't you put these on as well? You might just add a bit to their lustre,' I added flirtatiously.

She was quick to peel the wrapping off and I could see a glint in her eyes as she inspected each of the pieces, holding them at eye-level between her fingers.

'They are both identical,' I quipped. 'You can look at any one and decide whether you like them.'

'I know, silly,' she said, reaching out to garland me with her arms. 'Wait here,' she added, rushing out of the room only to return few moments later. She had a small packet in her hand which she handed over to me saying, 'And just so you don't feel left out, you can wear this.'

I nearly jumped out of my shoes as I saw an Omega watch staring back at me from inside the packet I had just opened. I wasn't much of a watch person and yet I could tell that it was an exquisite timepiece, one that would have set her back by at least twice my monthly paycheck. 'Wow, it is an Omega. It must have been expensive. How much did it cost?' I shot out involuntarily.

I agree, it wasn't one of my best reactions, but it was only a reaction for God's sake – sudden and impulsive. Of course I had every right to be concerned about the substantial dent in our finances that the watch would have caused, but till then that concern hadn't even erupted in my mind. My statement was a simple acknowledgment of the watch's magnificence and a natural curiosity to know its worth, nothing else. And yet Shalini's retort left me wondering if I had committed a cardinal sin by uttering those words.

'Why do you always… always… have to be so hard-headed? It is our first anniversary and I got you something that I wanted you to have. Yet all that you are concerned about is its price,' she nearly screamed, seething with anger. 'And just so you don't suffer sleepless nights, it isn't your money that has gone into buying it. I took the money from Dad.'

And that did it for me. I was incensed not only by her interpretation of my words, but also the revelation that she had been taking money from her father. It was a blow to my vanity and I couldn't take it lying down. We kept screaming at each other like a pair of mad wolves and eventually, when we were too tired to continue shouting, we retired into separate rooms. The dinner reservation was a failed plan by then.

In short, Shalini and I were thinking, behaving and living on two separate planes which did not converge. The more I thought about our situation, the more it appeared to be my fault. After all, it was I who had changed and not Shalini. But wasn't it only natural for one to mature slightly after tying the marital knot, I would justify to my own self.

I needed to make her understand that life wasn't the same anymore. Marriage came with a set of responsibilities and unless both of us rose to accept them, the crevices that had surfaced within us were only likely to widen. I tried to speak to her on a few occasions but always in vain. When things were going fine she would simply refuse to acknowledge the existence of any problems and when we were on warpath, well, we were on warpath. The possibility of a sane discussion then was as unthinkable as India and Pakistan behaving as friendly, considerate neighbours.

So, when our second anniversary offered an opportunity to steer our relationship clear of its blow hot, blow cold mode, I grabbed it with open arms. I took a couple of days off from work and combining it with the weekend to follow, booked for us a three-night holiday in Goa. Shalini, as expected, was extremely excited about the plan. And if the warmth she had begun to exude, her attempt to prepare bed-tea for me being a case in point, was anything to go by, I was certainly heading in the right direction.

We were booked on an afternoon flight from Mumbai and by the time we reached our resort near the Calangute beach, a scenic but long drive from the Dabolim airport, the sun was already signing off for the evening. Rushing through our check-in formalities, we headed for the beach to catch the red ball of fire ease itself into the vast expanse of water. Sunset in Goa is unlike any, especially when cherished while sipping a glass of Coconut Frappe, a rum-based cocktail. The experience was truly surreal and instinctively Shalini's hands slipped into mine and her head rested itself on my shoulder. That night we made love with a passion that I thought had evaporated from our midst.

The morning of our anniversary was mostly a laid-back one with an early morning stroll on the beach, a sumptuous breakfast and retiring to the room to cuddle off to sleep. We had both refrained from indulging each other with gifts, a learning from our last anniversary. We slept through the day, skipping lunch and preferring instead to remain in each other's arms. It was then that I realised how much I had been missing Shalini despite breathing in the same air as her over the past several months.

Come evening and we began to get ready. She opted for a comfortable pair of slacks that caressed her shapely legs like a surgeon's gloves and a loose-fitting t-shirt. She had refrained from applying much makeup, and her hair, falling free on her shoulders, gave her an adorable school-girl look. High on life once again, we set out to celebrate two years of marital togetherness. The venue was one of the prominent lounge bars on the stretch along the beach.

We sat there, sipping our drinks, reminiscing the times gone by and observing others – What they were wearing? How they spoke? And, to the best of our crooked imaginations, who was it that they had accompanied to the city that is sometimes referred to as the city of sins? It was just like the old times once again, and I couldn't help feeling pleased with myself on the decision to come to Goa. Only, I had no way of knowing then that my happiness was to be merely a fleeting one.

'Surprise,' I heard someone scream out.

I craned my neck to see a bunch of people, five in all, three men and two women, heading animatedly towards our table. I could recognise them all. Ishita's frame was unmistakable and the others were their common friends – Shalini's and Ishita's – that I had met sometime or the other while accompanying Shalini for her get-togethers.

I had been bumping into Ishita fairly regularly by virtue of her being Shalini's best friend, but after her break-up with Poka, which happened around the same time that Shalini and I decided to take the marital plunge, a certain degree of hesitation had crept up between us. I knew that the break-up was inevitable and that it had neither left Poka nor Ishita heartbroken, but I felt awkward in regarding her with the same blitheness as earlier. Perhaps the only party impacted by their ever so imminent break-up had been yours truly.

As the group wished us on our anniversary, handing us bouquets that they had brought, shaking my hands and hugging Shalini, I was left pondering about the story behind their sudden appearance in Goa, a city separated from Mumbai by over 500 kilometres. Not only that, they had landed up at the precise place where Shalini and I were, and the bouquets were a dead giveaway that they had been expecting us to be there. If this was a coincidence, I was the Great Wall of China.

The mystery began to unravel once the intruders joined us and had happily guzzled their first round of drinks. Apparently, 'the gang' had been planning a holiday for a while and when

Shalini told them about our plan to visit Goa, it ignited their thoughts into instant action. Shalini, of course, had been left out of the planning since the sudden ambush was to remain a surprise for her. During the day, Ishita texted her to check how the day was unfolding and what plans we had for the evening. Shalini inadvertently revealed the name of the lounge we were heading to and the rest was history.

Shalini was truly excited by the sudden and unexpected arrival of her friends. I must confess, I wasn't bothered either, at least not in the initial part of the evening. Their sudden accession had surely added a spark of life to our otherwise quiet table, but as time continued creeping into later hours, I realised that this was not what I had bargained for.

The carousal, incessant bickering and meaningless laughter had brought my golden moments with my wife to a screeching halt. What made matters worse was that Shalini appeared to be enjoying the transformed scenery just as much, oblivious and indifferent to the fact that our time together had been brutally cut short by the intrusion. It was just a matter of time that I began to feel out of place in their company, like a grown up surrounded by a bunch of kids would feel.

Most of the gang, including Shalini, was completely high in some time. They had been sneaking out in twos and threes to share a joint and the marijuana mixed with liberal measures of alcohol had begun its telling. I chose to stay away from the weed. In fact I had rarely ever smoked up since I started working. The lack of spare time of course was a factor, but I seemed to have lost the inclination for it as well.

The din of their carousal had risen substantially and no sooner did one of the guys get up to shake a leg in the space between tables, others rushed in to join him. I was the only one left watching.

It was when Shalini, intoxicated and barely conscious, slumped against Varun while dancing, her hands around his neck and her abandoned head resting on his chest, that I decided I had had enough. I called for the cheque and brought the festivities to an end, spoiling their party just as they had spoiled mine. I drove Shalini back to the hotel, but she was in no position to talk. And by the time I got up the next morning, I had lost my inclination to bring up the matter and address it by way of a discussion. Ironic as it was, Shalini and Varun dancing together during her birthday celebrations from many years back had led us to profess our love for each other. Today the same act had ruthlessly murdered and buried a part of me.

It wasn't that I didn't trust Shalini. In fact, if there was one thing I could be sure of, it was her unfailing loyalty. I had no doubt whatsoever that she was as faithful as any sari-wearing, vermilion-smearing Indian housewife is to her husband. The problem was that she was married now and hence was not supposed to behave so uninhibitedly with other men. I had no problems if she kept male friends or if she went out partying with them, but drinking yourself out of your wits and landing up in their arms was an entirely different matter.

The intrusion didn't just end there. Her friends were in Goa for the weekend too and the unstated but obvious expectation Shalini had was that we would party with them for the last remaining night of our stay. I managed to save myself the effort by feigning a headache. I had failed miserably in making our second anniversary a memorable one and with that, in helping our married life back on its track. I returned to Mumbai with a heavy heart and dissolved myself in work once again.

Just when I had lost all hope on Shalini and resolved to permit our respective lives to take the courses they willed, nature hurled another opportunity our way. One evening, when I returned home, Shalini informed me that she had missed her periods. She sounded gloomy. I was ecstatic. A do-it-yourself pregnancy kit was quick to confirm my unrestrained delight and her worst fears.

Shalini was visibly scared. She wasn't ready for motherhood as yet, she claimed. I was however glad that she refrained from bringing up the idea of an abortion. I don't know how I would have reacted if she had, but my reactions couldn't have been very civil for sure.

I did all that I could to stand by her side in this momentous phase of our lives – counselling her on the positive aspects of childbearing (most of which she was quick to dismiss stating that pregnancy would leave her all fat and ugly), accompanying her during her visits to the gynaecologist and instilling confidence in her to break the news to her parents.

The last step I could have perhaps done without, for, the minute her mother heard the news, she decreed that Shalini be brought to Delhi at once. Some age old custom demanded that, I was informed, girls when pregnant should be staying in their parental home. I consented, not because her mother had said so, but because I thought it would be in Shalini's best interest and in the best interest of our unborn child.

I stayed back in Mumbai as my job didn't provide me with much of a paternity leave, but I would travel to Delhi and be on Shalini's side nearly every weekend. Her father had commissioned one of the best gynaecologists in the city for her, and upon my insistence, most of Shalini's tests were deliberately scheduled for days when I was around. I didn't want to miss any part of the experience. I was going to become a father - the thought never sank in fully and instead left me in a trance-like state for most of the long waiting period.

It was there, in the gynaecologist's clinic that I had my first brush with real magic. The ultrasound image of the fetus, a tiny little being living inside Shalini's stomach, was as magical as anything could ever be. As the doctor pointed out the unborn baby's miniscule limbs, enabling us to envisage clear shapes in the milky haze on the screen, I felt a tear drop surreptitiously escape my eyes. I turned to look at Shalini and her eyes were moist too.

This was the biggest test of our lives, one that Shalini and I were in together. And there was no way in hell that we were going to mess it up. Once within the comforts of the home she had grown up in, Shalini's inhibitions about motherhood faded out on their own. She too, like me, began waiting with bated breath for our big day, the day when our little bundle of joy would be in our arms.

During the weekdays, when I was in Mumbai, she would call me every evening to tell me about how the baby had kicked her or how she had felt something move inside her tummy. We were suddenly talking for much longer stretches than we had when we were present under the same roof and this augured well for our relationship. Mother Nature had taken over the task of ironing the creases from our relationship and she was doing a fantastic job of it.

And then Myra entered our lives - a tiny roll that the nurse came out of the labour room with and deposited in my arms. Both of us remained comatose for some time – Shalini under the influence of heavy sedatives, inside the labour room, and I with an overwhelming surge of extreme ecstasy, outside the labour room. Realising my situation, Shalini's mother gently picked up the bundle and turned to show it to her husband. As he looked at his granddaughter, scrutinising her as though she were a delicate piece of art, I thought I saw a hint of dampness in his eyes. So, my ever-so-formidable father-in-law was human after all.

Heeding the doctor's advice, I waited six long months before bringing Myra and Shalini back to Mumbai. In preparing for their arrival I had arranged for a full-time maid to assist Shalini in taking care of the baby. There was also a toy cabinet in pink plastic I had bought and stuffed with all the toys that my daughter would use for the first few years of her growing up. The pink of the cabinet interfered with Shalini's impeccable styling of our flat and I was somewhat fearful of her reactions when she saw it. But allaying my concerns, she simply pulled me with her left hand, clutching on to sleeping Myra with the right, and planted a kiss on my forehead.

Myra's arrival was a blessing in disguise for us in more ways than one. While I began reprioritising my engagements to ensure that I was spending as much time with her as I could, Shalini's reckless lifestyle gave way to a more responsible and calculated one. Though she did not put a complete stop to her outings, they were no longer a matter of priority for her. In fact it was seldom that she went out with her friends now, and when she did, she insisted that I accompany her. Mostly we went out as a couple and limited our indulgences to watching a movie or eating out instead of drinking or reckless partying. Myra had, within months of her arrival, brought us closer than we had ever been through the three years of our marriage.

The first perceptible word that Myra spoke was 'Papa'. I was elated and more so when, before long, it became apparent that the chance utterance was only a sign of her stronger allegiance with one among the two parents. Myra waited for me to return from office, restlessness creeping into her with the first signs of the sun going down, and clang on to me for the rest of her waking hours once I arrived. She would dine sitting in my lap and it were my cacophonic lullabies that lulled her to sleep.

Myra was her Papa's girl and there was no debating that. Sometimes when Shalini would try to get her to do something against her will – eat, sleep or take a bath – she would run to me and once in the safety of my lap, eye her mother teasingly. Folding her brows in feigned anger, Shalini would then threaten her. 'Go, stay with your Papa only now. Don't ever come back to me,' she would say. And Myra would lackadaisically smile at her, still clinging on to whatever part of me she had grabbed with her tiny hands. These and other such mother-daughter antics made me dote over them both.

Maybe it was I, who, absorbed in my bliss, had missed taking note of the warning signals or maybe it emerged unheralded, but there came a time when Shalini began to falter once again.

When Myra turned three, we shifted her from the playschool to the nursery section of a renowned school nearby. Our efforts in coaching her towards self-sufficiency had paid off and she was now comfortable in the company of the maid, who also doubled up as her babysitter when Shalini or I were not around. This once again left Shalini with enough free time on her hands.

It started slowly, as meetings or get-togethers with friends once or twice a month. I didn't think much of it. After all she was my wife and not a prisoner I had been assigned to watch. In fact, at some level I was even glad that she had started to move out of the house once again. I had no intentions of burying the independent, dynamic Shalini under the burden of marriage or motherhood, and when I saw her repossessing the reins of her life, I could see no cause for concern.

Then she started coming back with alcohol on her breath. I brushed that aside too. She was no longer breastfeeding Myra and a little alcohol was hardly reason enough for me to fret.

But Shalini's degeneration was rapid this time. By the time I could sense the threat, she was already beyond redemption. The frequency of her outings swiftly increased to two or three times a week and the states of inebriation in which she returned continued to worsen. Once again I attempted to engage her in conversation, counsel her on the potential implications of her lifestyle on our relationship and on Myra, but yet again I found her in a state of complete denial.

She was only having 'a little bit of fun', she claimed, and that she didn't see anything wrong with it. It was in the divergence of our definitions for excess that the root of our differences laid. 'I am not a child for God's sake. I am conscious of what I am doing and I know where to draw the line. So, please... just let me be,' she would say, bringing the discussion to an inconclusive end. I would be left chewing my words and wrestling with the demons of my own concerns.

Our marriage soon began to slip into the rut it had emerged from. Myra's arrival had already dented our physical relationship severely. We no longer had the privacy or the freedom to follow our carnal desires at will and resultantly our passionate endeavours had been reduced to almost once-a-week affairs. And now, with Shalini's recurrent absence, the situation had only worsened, making it an even scarcer engagement.

Her indifference towards us had begun to impact me emotionally as well. Whenever I would return home to find Myra cuddled up to sleep with the maid and Shalini missing from the scene, my blood would begin to boil. Sometimes I would vent out my anger and we would argue futilely but mostly I chose to keep my feelings bottled within me. It wasn't the best thing for a child to grow up around constantly bickering parents and this I used as a pretext to contain my fury whenever it began to flare up.

And then the telling blow came. I had returned from a two-day trip to Delhi. My work in Delhi had concluded earlier than expected, so I had advanced my return flight by a couple of hours. The airline, for once, had lived up to its committed schedule and I was home by five thirty that evening. Myra, who had been playing with the maid, was delighted to see me and her excitement only soared when I handed her the dollhouse I had picked up from a shop at the newly constructed Delhi Airport. Shalini was of course missing.

'Didi has gone out. She has said she will be back in time for dinner,' the maid offered, without me seeking an explanation.

It wasn't that I would have found Shalini waiting to greet me had I arrived by the flight I was originally booked on. In fact, I don't think she even knew the expected time of my arrival to begin with. This was just the zone of indifference that our marriage had slipped into and once again I was at a loss of courage and hope to be able to redeem it. I was happy at the few hours I was getting to spend with Myra and that was all I wanted to think about.

We played with the dollhouse, conjuring and enacting spontaneous stories of dolls that lived in it, laughing and rolling on the floor. We played with her other toys, insatiably soaking in the joys of the moment as the maid watched us from a distance, smiling at our antics. I would have preferred to have Shalini watching us instead.

Then we had our dinner, together, in the same plate. Myra insisting that I feed her with my hands and I obliging like a father was supposed to. We then cuddled up on the couch to watch TV. I wanted to catch the evening news, but it wasn't I who wore the pants in the house any more. We were soon watching a cartoon series with a bunch of extremely loud and, dare I say, irritating characters. I wondered why the more likable ones like Mickey Mouse and Donald Duck had decided to desert the present generation.

Somewhere around nine o'clock Myra fell asleep on the couch. I switched off the television and gently headed towards my room to take a shower and change. I had no heart to disturb the calmness layering her pretty face.

I was standing at the window buttoning my t-shirt when, by sheer chance, I saw a car stop at the main gate of our building and Shalini stepping out of it. I didn't intend to intrude, but from the second floor I had a pretty good view of the gate and, from where I was, I could clearly see the driver's face as he rolled down the window to wave at my wife. It was Varun. As Shalini stepped inside the gate, a visible stagger disturbing her walk, I felt my fists clench. We were back to where we had started from.

I took my time changing and when I emerged into the drawing room, Shalini was pulling her set of keys from the door and shutting it behind her. 'Hi, when did you return?' she mumbled, looking at me with bloodshot eyes, as she deposited her purse on the side-rack. I didn't bother with a reply.

Next, shifting her gaze to the couch she said, 'Oh, she's slept already!'

'Why didn't you shift her to the bedroom,' she said to the maid who was standing like a statue in one corner of the hall. Instead of wording a reply she stepped forward, intending, I presume, to carry Myra to her room. But Shalini's raised palm made her stop midway.

'Leave it, I will take her,' she said, sliding her hands under Myra to lift her. By now I had deposited myself on one of the side chairs and was a silent spectator to the happenings.

I can swear now, that I had felt an ominous stab in my heart the very instant that Shalini had picked up Myra. But it was just a flash, too quick for comprehension, and I remained seated without betraying a reaction. Perhaps I should have reacted. Perhaps I should have stopped Shalini. But all that is in the hindsight now.

Shalini took one step forward and in the second she swayed, losing her balance. 'Watch out,' I got up screaming, but by then the damage had been done. In a single flash, as she involuntarily reached for the wall with one hand for support, her grip on Myra loosened and her little body hit the floor with a thud. Head first.

I felt my sensibilities dissolve in Myra's deafening wail and then, unthinkingly, I drew my hand and allowed it to land across Shalini's exposed cheek. It was an instantaneous reaction, perhaps fuelled by the thoughts I had been feeding my subconscious, but one that I live to rue till this day. It was not only a cowardly act, but a highly deplorable one. I hated myself for having struck her, but the damage was done and there was no going back from it.

Shalini remained frozen, staring blankly at nothing in particular, as I reached out to pick up Myra. The injury wasn't grave, just a slight abrasion at the back of her head. It was the shock of the fall that had scared her into crying. In fifteen minutes or so, Myra was back to sleep. After carefully relegating her to her bed I retired to the bedroom, grappling with a mix of anger, anguish and guilt. Shalini never came into the room.

The next morning I emerged, having rehearsed the lines of apology I was going to say to her, only to find Shalini pulling out a trolley-bag from Myra's room. She looked right through me as she made for the drawing room to leave the bag there. I stood still, trying to comprehend what was happening. She then went into the other bedroom and within minutes returned with a suitcase tailing her.

'What is all this?' I asked as she made for the drawing room with the suitcase.

'We are leaving,' she returned, without even turning to look at me.

'Leaving for where? And who is this 'we'?' I demanded.

'Me and my daughter, we can't stay here anymore.' Her pitch was normal but there was a calculated coldness to her tone that made me shiver. However, a section of her statement had instantly drawn my attention.

'Your daughter? Don't forget that Myra is my daughter too and she is going nowhere. You can go wherever you please, but don't even attempt to take her with you,' I said. The very idea that Shalini had intended to take Myra away from me had once again left me infuriated. I was almost snorting fire as I said these words.

Shalini was in no mood to relent either and we kept shouting and screaming at each other for God knows how long. I was certain that I wasn't going to allow Myra to leave the house and Shalini would have none of it. Sometime during our argument, Myra emerged from her room and was now staring at us with wide eyes and a look of fearful apprehension plastered on her face.

Shalini looked at her and then she looked at me. She repeated the act a couple of times before pausing to address me. 'Fine, you keep her here for now, but remember, I am not going to let my daughter stay with a loser like you. The biggest mistake I made was to go against my family and marry a conceited, cruel and covetous man like you. Myra is not going to stay with you and suffer for a mistake I made. I shall have her back, no matter what it takes,' she said.

I didn't respond. I simply waited for her to shove her belongings into the suitcase and head out of the door. Once she had stepped out I pushed the door after her, a little harder than I would have done otherwise.

I could feel a tendon throbbing near my right temple and holding my head between my hands I slumped down on the couch. The happy world I had so painstakingly put together had disintegrated all of a sudden, just like that, and I wasn't going to have another shot at restoring it.

Seven

In real time, I had had plenty to complain apropos Shalini and her attitude towards our marriage, but since her departure, with each passing day my memories had begun to distort. Like a pebble deposited in a riverbed, time was steadfastly eroding the rough edges from my reminiscences, leaving behind a smooth tender residue from the days gone by.

It was something like our days in school – we hated every bit of the time spent while still on the school roster, and later on, once monsignor time had worked on our memories, those very moments invariably became our most cherished ones. Only my mental metamorphosis with regard to Shalini's memories was much brisker.

In less than a week from the day she left, I was missing her so much that my resolve of not taking the initiative for reconciliation had sailed out of the window. Trampling over my pride (misplaced albeit), I dialled her mobile number, patiently listening to the rhythmic ringtone, only to be informed by an utterly mechanical voice that my call had gone unanswered. Not having any compelling reasons to disbelieve the voice, I hung up somewhat disappointed. But now that I had succeeded in overcoming my inhibitions once, my attempts in reaching out to her only intensified. I tried reaching her several times, to be greeted by the same mechanical voice always. Shalini wasn't particularly keen on engaging in dialogue with me, I gathered.

I even tried her Delhi landline number a few times, once tutoring Myra to do the talking even, only to be told by an unusually curt housekeeper that 'Didi' was not in and that she would be informed about the call when she returned. The housekeeper proved no better than the mechanical voice as far as curbing my curiosity was concerned. If his claims were to be believed, he didn't know where 'Didi' was or when she would return or what had she said when he informed her of my previous call. So thorough was his training that had I tried asking him his name he would have feigned ignorance on that as well, I was certain.

I would specifically find myself stumped when Myra enquired about her Momma. I would give her some terribly concocted excuse about what was keeping Shalini back in Delhi and that she would return soon, my heart shrinking slightly each time I did so. Some part of me wanted Myra to question my reasons, to argue about the excuses I served her, but she never did. And the blind faith with which she accepted my words only made me cringe all the more. It was in anxious moments like these that I bombarded her with text messages, apologising to her, asking her to return, begging her let go for Myra's sake, but Shalini never replied. It was as if the shock from my reprehensible outburst had stunned her into a stone – cold, unresponsive and unfeeling.

And then I heard from her. It was precisely the thirteenth day since she had left when a courier delivery boy, after calling to check on my availability, arrived home and handed me a small packet. It was an unmarked envelope bearing only my address and the courier slip stapled to it had the letters D E L H I scribbled on it by someone who had absolutely no chance of making a career in calligraphy. Instinctively I knew that the packet was from Shalini. The somewhat peculiar medium notwithstanding, I was eager to hear from her and therefore, without wasting any time, I tore open the envelope.

I unfolded the letter and as I read its first few lines I felt my jaw dropping steadily till it was nearly resting against my chest. Each word staring back at me from the piece of paper seemed like a sharp needle waiting for its turn to puncture my flesh and bathe itself in my blood. The letter was from Shalini alright, if not directly, through a representative at least, but the message was unlike any I had ever imagined. It was a notice from the Delhi Family Court accompanied by a copy of the petition filed by Shalini's lawyer seeking annulment of our marriage. My heart thumping madly and my throat suddenly parched, I dropped on the couch, reading each hazy word, allowing it to have the precise impact that had perhaps been intended.

The notice appeared to be in a standard format, one that the courts would be dishing out in hundreds every day to couples eager to part ways, with references to the enclosed petition and asking me to present myself before the bench on a specified date. It was the petition that contained the real explosives and by the time I was done reading the six-page document, my rage had escalated to a zone where I was incapable of feeling anything. The loaded words too had lost their sting by now.

Among other things, the petition accused me of 'Inflicting physical and mental abuses with the intent of causing danger to life and health', distorting the turn of events in a manner that presented me as the reincarnation of the devil himself. 'Hit her repeatedly', 'left her crying in pain', 'tortured her, unmindful of the impression it would leave on their child', were some descriptions used to give the petition its intended character. Not only that, the petition also mentioned a number of petty arguments from the past, some that I could barely recall, blowing them out of proportion to paint a picture of Shalini as the hapless victim and I as her ruthless tormentor.

Some details in the petition were such that it wasn't possible for anyone (not even an imaginative lawyer) to write them without

Shalini's aid. With this realisation something snapped deep inside me, severing all bonds of the heart that had been preventing me from pulling away from Shalini.

If this was how she felt about me, she could never really have loved me. The petition had reduced her from being the mother of my child to a complete stranger, in my mind at least. Of course Myra was free to regard her the way she pleased and I didn't intend to interfere with that. Though I needed to come clean on the lies I had been feeding the little girl. Her mother had left for the good, unlikely to return anytime soon, and she had every right to know that. More importantly Shalini had flung a challenge at me and I needed to deal with it firmly. Her petition deserved a befitting reply and I pledged to myself that I would ensure it got one.

The next few months went by like a whirlwind, testing, trying and stretching me to the brink. But I was determined. I could not allow Shalini to have her way, her influential family and the notable law firm she had engaged notwithstanding. After some online research I got in touch with a prominent divorce lawyer in Delhi and contacted her to represent me. I was now visiting Delhi more frequently than I would visit the supermarket, sometimes to attend court hearings or else when summoned by my lawyer for a discussion or to complete the required paperwork.

It was in the courtroom that I first saw Shalini since the day she had left Mumbai. She looked an insipid shadow of her earlier self. Her acorn-brown salwar suit, the netted dupatta that ran neatly over her head and the continual crease on her brows gave her a stern and somber look, one that was a sharp contrast to the Shalini I had known. I glanced in her direction a few times but her eyes were avoiding me like the plague. It was as though she had turned totally blind to my existence. Oddly, I felt somewhat miffed by her indifference. Perhaps, despite the fact that we were in a courtroom, waiting for our respective lawyers to wage a war of words against each other, some part of me had yet not written her off completely.

The judge - a bespectacled, thickset man with fluffy white hair which gave the impression that he had a poodle permanently parked on his head – looked down at us from his vantage point. The courtroom was nothing like those I had seen in the movies. It was a large hall crammed with hundreds of people, nearly half of them clad in black coats, who were going about their separate discussions uninhibitedly, lending a continual buzz to the air. It was as if fifty different meetings were underway all at the same time and I was amazed as to how the judge managed to retain his sanity, let alone focus and deliver justice in the given setting.

Every now and then the bailiff would walk up a few paces and scream out a name, making the most Indian of them sound like they were of Scandinavian origin, and a bunch of people would walk up to the judge's podium to present their arguments. After a delay of almost two hours from the designated time, when our names were announced, Shalini and I approached the stand guided by our respective attorneys.

The judge, like the father-figure his appearance made him resemble, heard both of them intently before turning his attention towards us – Shalini and me. 'Both of you have your entire lives ahead of you. Are you sure this is not a decision made in haste and one which you will live to regret later? You might still want to give the relationship a bit of time and see if the differences can be sorted out?' he enquired solicitously.

'Your Honour, we have filed the petition seeking annulment of the marriage on grounds of cruelty. The differences between my client and her husband are irreparable and there is no scope for them to be sorted out,' Shalini's lawyer interjected.

The judge looked at him and for once I thought that he would have him locked up in contempt of the court, but he did not. Instead he nodded sympathetically and turned to face Shalini once again. 'Do you share the opinions of your Counsel?' he asked. Shalini nodded in the affirmative.

'Well, in that case, I would suggest that the Counsels sit together with their clients and try and arrive at a settlement on the matter. It is in the best interest of both parties as well as the honourable court that the marriage be annulled on mutually agreed terms. The next date for your hearing will be ......,' the judge said, pausing to sift through a register and announce a date.

'Both of you come across as sensible individuals and I would have appreciated had you agreed to give your marriage another chance. However, I hope that you are able to arrive at some common ground to make your separation a cordial one,' he added, before returning his attention to the open register on his desk. The constant pitter-patter from the court reporter's typewriter ended abruptly and the bailiff stepped forward to announce another set of names. It was time for us to recede from the stand.

The judge came across as a nice old man. Perhaps too nice for the present day, for, it was only a matter of weeks before his hopes of awarding us a decree of separation on cordial terms were thwarted. The bone of contention was Myra, our little princess. While, handing over Myra's custody to Shalini was inconceivable for me, it was just as unacceptable for Shalini to let go of her daughter. The impasse was unbreachable and we were once again knocking the courtroom doors hoping that justice would be upheld, our respective definitions of the word not only divergent, but diametrically opposite.

The divorce proceedings were ugly, and that would be an understatement of the extreme order. The judge went on awarding dates after dates to the case, and both set of lawyers, proficient and skilled in what they did, left no stone unturned to establish the incompetence of the other party over the one they were engaged to represent. Matters to have unfolded within the confines of our drawing room, sometimes the bedroom even, were unabashedly discussed and argued, often leaving me with a sense of loathing for the woman I had once loved. It was Shalini who was bent upon making a mockery of our days together, wasn't she?

I would have given up if I could; the grief was too much to endure. But the stakes had been upped in the last hand. It was Myra I was fighting for, and for her sake, I could readily carry myself to the gallows if it ever came to that.

In these trying times the one pillar of support standing steadily by my side and urging me on was Myra. Yes, the same little girl who one would associate better with blackmailing me into buying her an ice-cream rather than bolstering my resolve in the sort of situation I was faced with. But then, aren't we grown-ups usually guilty of undermining the cognitive and perceptive abilities of children?

When I told Myra that her mother had left us for good and she wasn't likely to return anytime soon, her reaction left me baffled. Unperturbedly she asked, 'But why doesn't she want to stay with us?' There wasn't an iota of agitation or impatience in her voice. It seemed as if she had never really fallen for my excuses to explain Shalini's absence.

'She wants to stay with you baby. She loves you. It is Papa that she is angry with and so she has gone to stay at Nanu's place in Delhi,' I explained.

'If she is angry, why don't you go there and make up with her? She can come back home then.'

'I tried Beta, but she won't listen to me. She doesn't want to come back here. Instead she wants you to go to Delhi and stay with her.'

She listened intently, as any full-grown person would, and after a momentary pause she said, 'I won't go to Delhi. I will never leave you Papa. You are the best Papa in the whole world.' Her tranquil tone and calm composure as she uttered those well deliberated words, proved sharper than a blade's edge. The innocent assertion of her kinship was overwhelming and I felt an involuntary stream of tears trickle down my eyes.

'Don't cry Papa, crying will lead to creases on your face and you will grow old early,' she said, using her little hands to wipe my tears. She had only returned one of my own arguments that I often relied on to keep her from crying. But coming from her, the words seemed to adorn a completely new meaning. Still struggling to get a grip on my frantic emotions, I picked up Myra in my arms and held her close to my heart. Nothing was going to take her away from me. Not Shalini, not her lawyers, not the judge, not anyone.

Meanwhile, the courtroom drama continued unabated with the respective lawyers doing everything in the book to portray the other party as the villain of the piece. I am not sure as to which of the two sides managed to prove their point, but one thing they jointly managed to establish, beyond any reasonable doubt, was that Shalini and I were done with each other. Our marriage had crumbled like a wall of dominoes and there was no setting it right from where it now stood.

Gradually the focus of the debate moved towards Myra and the black-coated folks shifted their arguments to how it was in the best interest of the child to stay with her mother or her father, depending on the faction they were representing. It was once again a futile exercise, with both sides teeming with arguments to support their cause, but none compelling enough to make the old man on the chair make a decision.

My instructions to my lawyer were very clear: I could part with all my worldly belongings – the house, the car, all the money I had in the bank – things I could regain by working harder, I was prepared to slog it out for the rest of my working life if required, but not Myra. And going by the vigour and passion that Shalini's counsels displayed, their motivation to get Myra's custody for their client was just as compelling. Somewhere along the barrage of reasoning and legal precedents, the judge's patience eventually wore off and he ordered Myra to be presented in court during the next hearing.

I must confess I did use my access to Myra to my advantage once I learnt that her testimony would possibly form the ground for the judge to pronounce his judgment. I counselled her on the ways of the courtroom, apprised her of what to expect and what not to, and I helped her rehearse the answers to a set of questions my lawyer had provided me with well in advance. Myra went about it all with a sense of allegiance and responsibility that left me in little doubt about how she would fare. And on the appointed day she did not disappoint me.

While she dealt with the questions the judge and Shalini's counsel posed to her with remarkable dexterity, the highlight for me was the moment that Myra entered the courtroom and her eyes met Shalini's. She instantly averted her gaze and I felt her grip on my hand tighten slightly.

The distress I saw on Shalini's face, as she continually tried to catch Myra's attention, failing miserably each time, filled me with a soaring sense of perverse pleasure. It was poetic justice of sorts. She was getting the same treatment of indifference that she had meted out to me not very long back. I was aware even then that my feelings were not something I could take pride in, but I couldn't help a part of me from giving a content smile.

'You don't need to be afraid of anyone or anything. This is entirely your choice. Only you can decide who you want to stay with… your Papa or your Momma, no one else. If anyone has forced you or threatened you into saying what you just said, please tell me my child and I promise you that no one will be able to harm you in any way. You have nothing to be afraid of,' the old judge said to Myra. His tone was sincere and the concern in his voice was as genuine as the white shrubbery growing on his head.

As an answer to his last question, Myra had just expressed her desire to stay with me rather than Shalini and expectedly Shalini's counsel had burst out like a firecracker on a short fuse. He had accused me of 'brainwashing' Myra, 'influencing' her, and what not; prompting the judge to make sure that the child had given her statement free from any duress.

'No one has forced me Sir. I want to stay with my Papa only,' she said with the natural guilelessness of the child that she was.

Though the judge reserved his order for the next hearing, I knew that Myra had dealt the telling blow. The battle was over and no one was going to take her away from her Papa.

On the day of the verdict, I came straight to the courthouse from the airport. I was brimming with excitement, like a victor raiding his acquired territories to collect the spoils. Myra was back in Mumbai. I saw no point in subjecting her to unnecessary travel. Moreover, there was the latent fear somewhere within my heart – what if, by some stroke of misfortune, the judge decided to hand her over to Shalini? I hadn't consciously deliberated over such an eventuality and didn't even know what I would do if it were to actually unfold, but I had decided to keep her away from the epicentre of the proceedings nevertheless.

But once the judge summoned us to his chamber, I realised that I wasn't the only one who had anticipated my victory. Shalini's counsel too had sensed the eventuality and was geared up to make my sailing as rough as he possibly could. Picking up from some previous arguments that my counsel, at my behest of course, had made in the courtroom, he drove a hard bargain, seeking just an ounce or two short of the moon as an upfront lump-sum settlement in lieu of alimony. He asked for all that I had once offered – my house, my car, a sum of money that would leave my bank account barely breathing – and I obliged unflinchingly.

Eventually I walked out of the courtroom a happy man, the judge having granted Myra's custody to me. Of course, Shalini had the option of contesting the verdict in a higher court, an option I was sure she would exercise, but until that happened, I was the legally appointed guardian for my daughter. It was a victory, not only for me but for Myra as well and I couldn't help but bask in its glory.

The streets of Delhi, as I made for the airport, with their swaying trees, cheerfully honking vehicles and teeming faces of passersby appeared to be celebrating my victory in its own offbeat manner. It must have been the elation I was ballooning with, for the very character of the city roads that now seemed in harmony with my triumph had often served me as a reason for discontentment in the past.

The faces I saw on the pavements and crossing the streets had usually been an odd assortment of purposelessness, mundanity and arrogance to me, and the ceaseless honking, well, the lesser said about that the better. But not anymore. In the reflective existence of my mind, they were all a part of the larger good. They were sights and sounds that made life what it was – an imperfect painting of kaleidoscopic hues.

The little time I had before boarding the flight, I expended sipping an aerated beverage at the Business Class lounge. I had a conspicuous smirk affixed on my face and I made no efforts to wipe it away. For once I was content to let my mind pleasure from the slight indulgences I had made a habit of ignoring.

Once inside the plane and gently ushered to my allotted seat, I reached out for a business magazine from the pile ahead of me, one that had nearly half-a-dozen world leaders staring back at me from its cover. The World Economic Forum meeting was underway and though I wasn't really expecting any conceivable outcomes that could turn the nose-diving world economy on its head, it was an occupational necessity for me to remain abreast with such crucial events. I had only just begun reading the cover story when suddenly an airhostess, following a glass of water she had just doused me with, landed squarely on my lap.

I was livid, possessed by the instinctive, conceited fury of the privileged Business Class traveller. Her carelessness could perhaps have gone down as a mistake or an error had it occurred in the Economy section of the cabin, but here, in the zone of the privileged, even the slightest of blunders was intolerable. She deserved to be reprimanded and I was in no mood to allow her a reprieve. It took me a little time before I could find the right words, civil and yet effective, to express my displeasure. But by then she had mumbled something and vanished behind the curtains that separated the passenger area from the in-flight pantry.

She emerged moments later, holding a bunch of tissues to clean up the mess she had caused, and that was when I saw her in entirety. She wasn't anything astounding, unlike the girls who grow up dreaming about becoming a skimpily-clad month in some collectible calendar. She was just a simple girl of normal built with sharp features and a dried-apricot complexion, like the many you come across in the vicinity of any university or college campus of the country. It was her eyes that made her different. The sincerity and unflustered manner with which they looked back prevented me from voicing the words that were billowing at the tip of my tongue. Impulsively I returned her smile and excused her – Avantika, the letters on her breast-plate read.

Don't get me wrong, I wasn't smitten by her or anything of the sort. Hell, I was a married… correction, divorced… man who had not yet gotten over celebrating the fact that the court had awarded him his daughter's custody. It was just that the look on Avantika had made me backtrack from my intended course, a somewhat unusual occurrence.

The typical male in me, an attention-seeking egoist, had made me read deep into her dispositions, beyond the intended perhaps, and I had allowed myself to be swayed by what I assumed to be the extra courtesy she was extending towards me. But this was only momentary, for the time the flight remained airborne and she remained within my sight. Avantika was soon out of my mind and my life, for the time being at least.

A couple of days later, when I bumped into her again at a Mumbai mall, almost as remarkably as our first meeting, once again I thought it to be coincidence doing an extended shift.

I had no way of knowing then that the very girl, Avantika, would soon become such an integral part of my life that I would be wandering about the country's length in trying to locate her.

Eight

'Rahul, the boss wants to see you.' I was informed by Stella, my boss's assistant, as I walked past her desk.

'Sure,' I said, revealing the special smile I reserved for Stella every morning. Uneasily I walked to my seat, glanced at my watch and plugged in my laptop. It was quarter past ten. I was late yet again. Myra, as she often did, did not want to go to school and the maid's best efforts in convincing her were falling on deaf ears. I had to intervene, steering past her pretentious headache, and persuade her to get ready in time for the bus.

This however couldn't be the reason for the boss wanting to see me. We consultants did not operate on a nine-to-six shift and it was commonplace for people to trickle into office all through the day. And if it offered any consolation, I had left office only around nine thirty the previous night. Deciding to put an end to the instinctive speculations in my mind, I walked up to the boss's cabin, sparing another smile for Stella, and knocked gently on the glass door.

'Come on in,' Prabhakar said, looking up from the laptop screen and adjusting his spectacle frame ever so slightly. 'Take a seat.'

The look on his face was solemn and the unease I had felt when Stella told me about his wish to see me had now taken the form of a knot and was rolling about somewhere within my belly. I returned his gaze wordlessly. He knew why I was there; he was the one who had summoned me after all. So, instead of a stupid sounding, 'You had called me?' I opted to wait for him to break the suspense.

He spoke soon enough. 'Rahul, we have a situation on our hands. A grave one,' he began, pausing to allow the severity of his words to sink in. I continued looking at him heedlessly.

'One of your clients has complained about you,' he continued, naming one of the biggest public sector clients I was working with. 'They claim that you have leaked some confidential information to their contractors and that they have adequate proof to substantiate this allegation.'

'What rubbish!' I nearly screamed.

'I know, I know…,' Prabhakar said, lifting a hand and nodding his head in a gesture meant to ask me to keep my calm. 'We have been working together for a while and I know you better than to believe such bull shit allegations. You don't have to convince me about the baselessness of the accusations Rahul.'

And just as my breathing was returning to normal, he spoke once again. 'But the problem is that he has written to Mr. Sinha directly and I was informed of the issue by Mr. Sinha himself. I told him exactly what I believe, that there is no way you could have done such a thing, but you know how it is, right? It is the clients that we make our living out of, and a client's word is not open to scrutiny, investigation or challenge. If a client wants you out, there is little anyone else can do.'

Prabhakar continued with his monologue, but his words were falling on deaf ears now. Though I was sitting across his desk, my mind was at work elsewhere. The mention of Mr. Sinha, our managing director, the very man who had got me the job to begin with, had set alarm bells ringing in my head. I had realised that this - my discussion with Prabhakar - was merely a ruse and that within a matter of minutes, an hour at best, I would be walking out of the office an unemployed man.

'You understand, right? There is nothing personal to this. You have been a fantastic resource and I have no doubts that you will be successful wherever you choose to go from here,' Prabhakar was speaking. I nodded understandingly and reached out to pick up the envelope that he had just pushed towards me. 'This has your settlement cheque… You can leave the laptop and the Blackberry with Stella once you have cleared your desk.'

I nodded and got up, the non-descript envelope dangling insouciantly between my fingers, and made for the glass door.

'It appears you have ruffled some serious feathers here buddy… Anyway, wish you the best for wherever you decide to go,' I heard Prabhakar say after me, a sincere tone dabbing his voice, but I did not take the pains to turn back and face him.

I returned home feeling miserable and depressed. I had never thought that Shalini could stoop to such low levels. She was vengeful alright, but she also knew what my job meant to me. It was like a backbone for me, my only source for the money I desperately needed for Myra's and my upkeep. How could she be so brutal and insensitive so as to deprive us of our very foundation?

Once home, I headed straight inside, into my bedroom, and dropped myself on the bed. The sun was out, its rays squeezing in through the window and claiming a rectangular portion of the bedroom floor. It would still be a few hours before Myra returned from school and that was about all the time I had to think through the unexpected calamity and come up with a plan to emerge from it. More importantly, I had to get a grip on myself by then. I was sure I looked like a man who had been picked up by a tornado and released abruptly amidst a shower of debris and rubble.

My situation was genuinely precarious. The court had given me a month to vacate the house and hand over its possession to Shalini. I wasn't left with enough cash in the bank to pay even for the deposit of a decent rental flat and I had embarked upon the house-hunt hoping to raise the required funds through a personal loan. And now, with my newfound status of an unemployed youth, I was unlikely to remain a favoured customer for any bank, especially when it came to extending credit. The cheque against my final settlement with my erstwhile employers could plug this deficit, but that would have left me with absolutely nothing to survive on.

I had to get myself a job urgently, but that was not going to be easy either. I had been terminated from my job and not asked to resign from it. The implication being that my relieving letter, which any new employer would ask for before hiring me, mentioned that I was 'terminated' due to 'integrity issues', a revelation that was bound to bring the hiring process to a shuddering halt. Shalini had not only left my arms tied, she had ensured that they were duly amputated.

I was so engulfed in my thoughts that the sudden ring of my mobile phone left me startled. Avantika, the flashing display read. The last thing I wanted to do then was engage in frivolous banter with a girl I had only met twice. I grabbed the instrument with the intention of disconnecting the call, but on a sudden inexplicable impulse, ended up receiving it.

'Rahul? This is Avantika. Hope you haven't forgotten me?' I heard her measured voice on the line.

'No, no, how can I dare to forget you? And even if I managed to, somehow, I am sure you will hunt me down and tackle me to the ground or douse me with a watering hose… No?' It wasn't easy for me to sound normal when the world around me was crumbling, but now that I had opted to take her call, courtesy demanded that I humour her.

'Very funny! Anyway, how have you been? And how is Myra? Does she remember me?'

I have been at my rocking best; it feels like I have won an Olympic medal, a Nobel Prize and the cricket World Cup, all within a span of a few hours, I felt like saying. But I checked myself and instead returned. 'She is well... off to school now, and it is highly unlikely that she would have forgotten the aunty who shares her strange taste in movies. There are not many grown-ups who fit that bill you know! How about you, how have you been?'

'Oh, I have been good too. Was here in your city, so thought I will check on you guys...,' she said, allowing her words to tail.

'That's nice! So, till when are you in Mumbai? And if you don't have any special plans for the evening, why don't you drop by. You can then check for yourself whether Myra remembers you or not,' I offered.

The invite wasn't a conscious one. It was plain rhetoric, a polite response to the knowledge that the caller happened to be in the same city as me, and I was somewhat taken aback when Avantika took me up on the offer. I got a feeling that she had been waiting for me to utter those words, and instantly I felt my chest swell by a couple of inches. The typical male within me was reacting, prohibiting my brain from doing the thinking, and before I knew I had fixed up for Avantika to have dinner with us.

She arrived shortly after six, looking her usual serene self that I was slowly coming to get accustomed to. She was wearing a white Lucknawi suit, one that caressed her slender frame blithely and accentuated her sharp features and dusky complexion. Myra was excited to see her and allowed me only the exchange of basic pleasantries before ushering Avantika to her room.

The two continued playing for better part of the evening with my presence reduced to merely a peripheral one. Myra was excited, perhaps at having found a new playmate, but Avantika appeared no less animated. It was as though Myra's company had transported her back to her own childhood. Myra had a zillion things to show to her, from her sketch book to her dollhouse and her favourite dress to the photographs from her last birthday, and Avantika matched each item with a unique expression of indulgence. It was only when the maid announced dinner that their frolic ended, with a fair bit of reluctance, I might add.

'What happened? You are not your usual self today. Is something wrong?' Avantika enquired as we sat gorging on the sumptuous meal that the maid had put together with slight help from a nearby restaurant catering to home orders. It was more an observation than a question and I had little difficulty in evading it. However, I couldn't help feeling surprised, pleasantly of course, at her accurate assessment of the situation despite the limited interaction we had managed through the evening.

A little after we were done with dinner, Myra, at my behest, grudgingly dragged herself to her room. She wanted to sit with us and chat with Avantika Aunty, but it was way past her bedtime and she had school the next morning, unlike me who had nothing better to do. Aware that Avantika might want to leave anytime soon and not wanting to let go of her, partly because I was enjoying her company and partly because I didn't want to be left alone to struggle with the demons of my thoughts, I poured us a glass of wine each.

We parked ourselves on the sofa and after a few sips from her glass Avantika posed her question again, the same one I had managed to evade at the dinner table earlier. However, this time the determination in her voice told me that an escape was highly unlikely if not impossible. I began to talk, starting from the happenings from earlier that day, tracing the roots of my problems to my bitterly-fought divorce with Shalini, right up to the early days of our married life when the seeds of discord had begun to sprout.

I would have spoken non-stop for an hour, or even more, and Avantika sat there, quiet and brooding, listening to every word I said. I don't know what made me open up to her, perhaps the wine, or the fact that the turmoil brewing within me desperately needed a release, or even some twisted need for sympathy, but in the end I was glad that I had let it all come out. The outburst hadn't alleviated my problems or equipped me any better to handle them, but I was feeling much lighter in the head already.

'Sometimes God creates such situations to test us. Don't worry, you will emerge out of this a much stronger man,' she said, resting her hand over mine in a reassuring gesture.

Her words meant nothing. They were like an overarching sermon, some abstract patter of spirituality which had little practical relevance. I should have cringed at them. I normally would have too, but for Avantika. She sounded like she actually believed what she was saying, and this, to me, was oddly heartening. I nodded and she continued for a while more, uttering words with the singular purpose of comforting and encouraging me. I could see through her intent and yet I was helpless in preventing the words from having their intended effect.

She left soon after, blatantly refusing to allow me to drive her to her hotel.

'You are drunk, you can't drive. I will hail an auto,' she said with a sense of finality.

'Drunk? Hell… I have only had a few glasses of wine. If you call this getting drunk, wait till you actually see me drinking. I am alright, don't worry, I will drop you back,' I reasoned.

'No!' she nearly screamed. 'Two glasses of wine or an entire bottle, you are not driving under the influence of alcohol and that is final. I don't understand how you can afford to take life so lightly. Grow up, if not for your sake then for your daughter's.'

She was making a mountain of a molehill, and I was in no mood to argue. So I settled for walking her to the main road and helping her hail an auto-rickshaw instead. Girls, sometimes they can get hyper over the slightest of things, I thought, shrugging, as the little yellow-black vehicle sputtered down the empty road.

If ever I thought that the auto had succeeded in taking Avantika away from my life and its problems, I couldn't have been further from what was to unfold. The evening had only served to ease her into my life and from that day on Avantika was always there around Myra and me, whether in person or in spirit.

It seemed that by confiding in her I had established some sort of a bond, a mystical connection, which left her feeling responsible for me. She began by calling to check on me, informing me of relevant job opportunities I could explore, mostly from some of the leading job portals that I had already subscribed to. Though the tips, I knew, were of little use to me, I never let that be known to her as it was her thoughtfulness and tenacity I was moved by.

Soon she was visiting us pretty regularly, spending time with Myra, accompanying me in my house hunting expeditions and counselling me on my career, or the lack of it. I had no reasons to dissuade her. In times like these a shoulder to lean on is all one seeks, and Avantika was a steady support that I was slowly and unwittingly getting habituated to.

When the opportunity emerged, a Business Development role with an ecommerce start-up that promised only a fraction of my erstwhile salary, it was she who counselled me into taking it up. Despite posting my resume on all conceivable job sites and even applying directly on the websites of every consulting firm I could think of, I was getting nowhere. Not a single interview call. Not even a call from a recruitment firm wanting to discuss my profile. Resultantly my frustrations were mounting by the day and just when I was on the verge of writing myself off as a failure, I received a request to connect from an old acquaintance on a networking portal I had posted my profile on.

Arden was a senior from my M.B.A. institute, and as far as I could recall, his campus placement had been with a leading IT services company. I vaguely remembered having heard that he had quit his job to start something on his own, but I wasn't too sure. And now, when I saw his profile with the word 'Managing

Director' underlining his name, a solitary ray of hope emerged from the screen to soak me. I wrote to him and received a prompt reply. He remembered me too. The signs were promising.

On the following day I was sitting in his cabin, discussing with him the business model for his setup and keeping my eyes out for any possible crevice where I could fit in. The model was simple: The company got into arrangements with leading brands in the consumer space to purchase significant quantities of their products, those that the manufacturers were excessively stocked with, obtaining significant discounts against the voluminous purchases. These discounts were then passed on to consumers through their website, guaranteeing the lowest prices for the catalogued products. Business was picking up and, if Arden was to be believed, was all set to break even within the next fourteen months.

He even talked about the possibility of a venture fund picking up some stake in the company, but that prospect, I knew, was more an outcrop of the optimism that the new breed of entrepreneurs were identified with. I was more interested in the brass tacks, an immediate solution to my bread and bed problem, and so I brought it out on the table. I told him that I was keen to work with him, if an opportunity was available, giving him a broad summary of my situation.

He did have something, he said. It was a Business Development role, a position that was responsible for approaching brands and striking discount-based deals with them. The job was not up my alley, extremely menial in comparison with the projects I had handled for my erstwhile employers, but it was a job nevertheless. The issue however emerged when he mentioned the compensation he had in mind. It was less than half my last drawn salary. Of course, he was willing to part with 2% stake in the company, but that was like an egg that I could find myself waiting forever to hatch. The share could translate into anything of value if and only if the company made it big and managed to lure some venture fund to invest in it.

I had left Arden's office, promising to get back to him after giving the offer my due consideration. I was sceptical to take up the job since it would not only mean a substantial compromise in my manner of living but it would also set my career back by several years. For any new job I was to seek in the future, my present salary would be looked at as a yardstick, and if I agreed to such a substantial cut now, it was bound to stick with me for the rest of my life.

It wasn't an easy decision, and it was only with Avantika's sound reasoning and the fact that there weren't very many employers tussling to get their hands on me that I managed to make up my mind.

The implications were severe. I had to let go of my in-house maid for one. Over time, the maid had become like a family member to us. Myra was especially attached to her and the attachment had only grown post Shalini's departure from our lives.

I broke the news to her with a heavy heart and, handing her a few thousand rupees over and above the amount I owed her, a sum I wasn't then sure if I could afford, I bid her farewell. To my utter amazement her reaction to the news was uncaring and relaxed, as if I had only asked her to take a few days break. Perhaps the job market in their industry wasn't as tight as it was in mine, but I was glad that she reacted the way she did, for it helped me in pacifying my own feeling of guilt to some degree. It was only when she hugged Myra for the last time that I saw watery traces emerge in her eyes. Myra obviously wasn't told that she would never be seeing her Didi again.

The second casualty of my compromised financial condition was my affinity with the locality I lived in – Juhu, a premium suburb of the city. The focus of my house hunt was forced to shift northwards and eventually I zeroed in on a one-bedroom apartment in Borivali, a habited locality no doubt, but one that I had managed to remain oblivious to during all the years I had spent in Mumbai.

Avantika once again had a key role to play in preparing me for this deliberate downgrade in my living standards. She wasn't around when I had first seen the place, but later, when I told her about the apartment, especially the reasonable rent it was going for, she was quick to latch on to it. She dragged me along to see it for herself and thereafter, for the next two days, kept feeding me with its non-existent advantages.

It was only when I had professed my readiness to move into it that she relented, but only momentarily. Once we were handed over the flat keys, she buried herself in decorating it with inexpensive but stylish artefacts – so like Shalini, and yet, so much unlike her – and once again showering it with praises on how airy, spacious and beautiful it was. Mostly unmerited compliments meant solely for my consumption.

The house-shifting was a depressing and chaotic process, with the unpleasant task of sorting out and discarding items that we had piled up over the years and which our new dwelling was inept of containing, consuming a significant portion of my time. But I managed nevertheless, bracing the compromise with a tailored sense of optimism.

Even Myra, clearly the one most severely impacted by the relocation, did her best to hide her sorrows. Not once did she complain about leaving behind her friends, moving out of the room she had painstakingly decorated with drawings and sketches she considered her masterpieces or even about shifting to a school that hardly compared in size and stature to the one she had been attending. Myra had put up a face too brave for her years, and oddly, it was her compassion that pained the father in me the most. Whenever I saw her face, the twinkle in her eyes trying to conceal her ingenuous emotions, I felt an inexorable sting within my heart. I knew I had let her down and the burden of this was a devastating one.

Despite her efforts at feigning indifference, her distress with the unexpected course our lives had taken showed in her fading smile, the paleness which had swallowed her cheerful effervescence and the quiet reclusive child she had suddenly transformed into. She was no longer eager to go down and play with the other kids. Well, she didn't quite know the children in our new locality as yet. But the Myra of the past would have reached out and befriended them instead of keeping herself at bay. It was only when Avantika was calling that I got to see glimpses of Myra's earlier self and this made me eagerly await her visits.

I had conveniently relegated the alterations in Myra's demeanour to the sudden change of surroundings and assumed that, if left alone, it would only be a matter of time before she adjusted and settled into her own zone of comfort. But the truth - a ferocious, lurking monster – when it emerged, was far even from my scariest nightmares, let alone harmless assumptions.

One morning, while getting ready for school, Myra complained of dizziness and nausea. As I led her to the bed, slightly alarmed, I saw a red trickle emerge from within her nose. Instinctively I reached out to wipe it with my hand, only to find my fingers smeared with my daughter's blood. I was frozen stiff. Her nose was bleeding. In the few moments it took me to reclaim my bearings, the faint streak had broadened and the blood was threatening to touch her lips.

I lifted her off her feet and asking her to keep her head arched, rushed her to the bed. The bleeding ceased eventually, but not before it had nearly soaked two hand-towels and left me trembling like a leaf.

Towards the evening, when Myra got up from her sleep, feeling feeble and sapped, I took her to her regular paediatrician in Juhu. Financial snags or no, the one thing I wasn't prepared to compromise on was my baby's health. Myra deserved the best medical attention that money could buy and that she was going get irrespective of the circumstances.

The doctor, after interrogating us both about the history and intensity of Myra's condition, prescribed a couple of medicines and a blood test for the sake of diagnostic accuracy. Myra, like most children her age, was petrified of needles and it took a lot of patience, some cajoling and fair bit of pep talk before she allowed the nurse to go about her task. When we emerged from the clinic, her eyes were still red and swollen with all the tears she had shed and she wasn't talking to me, obviously holding me responsible for the torture she had undergone.

Once back home, the pills worked like magic and Myra regained her strength in no time. I was relieved and not having anyone else to share my reprieve with, I dialled Avantika's number.

'How did it happen? What did the doctor say? She must have hurt her nose somewhere. You should keep a closer watch on her,' she burst out hysterically on hearing about the bleeding nose. I smiled to myself. I could afford to do so, now that Myra had recovered. And no, I wasn't deriving some perverse pleasure out of the conversation; it was just that Avantika's concern was truly touching. I was only blissfully content about the affection and fondness for my daughter that her exasperated words implied.

She permitted me to hang up only once I had shared every minute detail with her, painting as much a picture of the proceedings as I could manage with mere words and responding to her volley of probing questions – What all did the doctor ask? How did Myra react to the sight of a syringe? Was it painful? Did she cry? How is she feeling now? Did you buy her a chocolate?

I slept peacefully that night, my conscious thoughts about Myra and Avantika tapering into a strange dream, one of the rare ones that I could vividly recall even after I was awake. I saw an enormous garden, one where flowers – red, yellow and purple, of a make I couldn't quite identify – covered the ground like a patterned carpet, and birds with brightly coloured feathers and melodious voices (one of them was even humming an A. R. Rehman tune) swooped over them lazily.

There was a lone human form in the distance, sprawled on the bed of flowers, gazing at the blue, cloudless sky. At first I couldn't recognise the individual. There was a cloudy screen preventing me from doing so. But as I focused my attention, the form began to drift towards the precinct of familiarity: a girl… a little girl… a little girl I knew from somewhere… a little girl I knew very well… Myra, my own little girl! Indeed, the girl was Myra and she was relaxing, soaking in the environs, peace and tranquillity writ all over her face.

Just then a slight movement drew my attention and what I saw left my heart pounding like an African drum. A ferocious creature, eyes smouldering red, and its black glossy skin gleaming slimily in the sunlight, was tiptoeing towards Myra. It was approaching her from the direction of her head, carefully avoiding the periphery of her vision. The beast walked on two legs, hunched slightly, and had a pair of thick wings protruding from its back, much like the aliens born to animation for being cast in one or the other Hollywood flick. Whatever it was, it intended to harm Myra, I could gather. She needed to be warned. Somehow! Anyhow!

I tried to scream, but my voice failed to reach my own ears. I tried to run towards her, but my feet seemed to have resigned from the services of my brain. The beast was now merely a leap away from Myra and I couldn't do anything to help her, to save her. I was breathing in gushes, concentrating, hoping that my limbs would heed to the frantic orders of my mind, but only to be greeted by further frustration. It was as if I did not exist at all. I wasn't a part of the frame. I could see them but as a mere spectator who had been denied any rights of interference.

Suddenly the beast stopped and eyed Myra, allowing its tongue to caress its ugly lips ever so slightly, before turning to look at me. Its amber eyes bore into mine and I was certain that it was mocking me. I tried once again to shake my limp body to life, but to no avail. I remained still, like a corpse. The beast then buckled its knees, looked greedily at Myra for the last time and jumped. I wanted to close my eyes in horror, but even that slight escape proved beyond my faculties.

And then, in a flash, a figure materialised from nowhere, nearly human, but for its glittering pink texture and the wing-like protrusions on its back. It landed right on top of Myra, using its hands and legs for support, ensuring that the little girl wasn't crushed under its weight. With one of its wings it veiled a startled Myra and with a flap of the other it met the beast midway through its jump. The impact was potent, sending the predator flying a few paces, to land with a thud on the flowerbed. The beast got up, eyed the intruder, who was now gnarling back at it ferociously, and stepping back, retreated to where it had emerged from.

Myra's saviour then turned to look at me and an instant flicker of recognition emerged. Crouching ahead of me, smiling slightly and still shielding my daughter was Avantika, in an angelic, never-seen-before avatar. I tried to say something but I am not sure if the words did come out, for this was the time that my sleep chose to desert me.

When I got up, I was sweating profusely and a damp puddle had formed on the bedsheet. I glanced to the side and at the sight of a peacefully asleep Myra I felt an intense wave of relief rush through me. Gently brushing my hand over her head, I closed my eyes once again. It was only a dream, bad or good, I could always deliberate later.

The next afternoon I was busy sending out some e-mails pending from the previous day when I received a call from Myra's doctor. 'Mr. Singh?' he enquired, and upon my confirmation and the exchange of basic pleasantries, he continued. 'Myra's blood test reports have come. The reports are fine except for one little thing. It isn't something you need be perturbed about but a condition you need to be aware of so that you can exercise the required caution. It would be good if you could stop by at the clinic on your way back home today. I will explain everything to you then.'

I was too stunned to probe further. Though he had said that it wasn't anything I needed to worry about, I couldn't prevent a sinking feeling from swelling up within me. There was a practiced calmness to the doctor's tone that I didn't like. I could almost visualise him conveying the news of one of his patient's demise to the aggrieved family in a similar voice.

Brushing off the warped thought, I shut down the laptop and made for Arden's cabin to inform him that I wouldn't be in office for rest of the day. Arden had been extremely sympathetic of my situation up till now, allowing me all the time I needed to sort out my life , and it pained me to draw the leash of his considerations any further. But there was no way I could bring myself to work after the conversation I had just had with the doctor.

I reached the Juhu clinic in a state of near trance, oblivious to the hectic pace with which the city went about, thinking only about Myra and praying to all the deities I had ever heard of for her well-being. I had never really been a firm believer in the power of the divine. I wasn't an atheist either, but just that I had been brought up on wisdoms of the Bhagwad Gita, and in accordance I preferred indulging myself in my Karma, the deeds I was obligated to do, rather than expending my energies in appeasing an unknown, unseen authority. But the stakes had suddenly upped themselves and when it came to Myra, any help, from any quarter, known or unknown, was more than welcome and I was even prepared to plead for it.

'Aplastic anaemia,' the doctor said. 'It is a rare disorder where the body's bone marrow doesn't make enough new blood cells.'

He went on uttering some gibberish about red blood cells, white blood Cells, Platelets, their expected lifespans etcetera, but I wasn't listening. His words were ringing like a gong near my ears and I was sitting across the table, staring at him like a zombie.

'Mr. Singh… Mr. Singh…,' the doctor's voice summoned me to reality after some time. 'As I was saying, we only suspect this condition and a few more tests will be required before we can say anything with certainty. Moreover, the condition is curable. In case of early detection, all she might need is a couple of weeks of medication and she will be perfectly alright. Don't worry yourself needlessly… Just bring her here at the earliest you can and we shall conduct the remaining tests.'

The doctor might say what he wished, but somehow I knew the results of the tests even before they were conducted. Suddenly, all those times that Myra had complained of headaches, breathlessness and an uneasy feeling within the stomach came back to me in a flash. Devastated from within, I left the clinic and headed home. I needed to see Myra urgently, be with her, embrace her and tell her how much her Papa loved her.

That night I called up Avantika once again. I didn't intend to, but as soon as I got down to telling her about my conversation with the doctor, the barrage containing my emotions broke down. I cried like a baby, sobbing and wailing, for who knows how long. She kept listening to me, patiently, slipping in an odd consolatory word every now and then, allowing me to vent all that I had been holding within.

'I am coming to Mumbai tomorrow,' she finally said. 'Don't worry Rahul, nothing will happen to Myra.'

Nine

If I were a superstitious man, I would have blamed Avantika's entry into our lives for the turmoil that followed. A bad omen, as they say. My job loss, the forced shift from a locality we were so accustomed to - Myra and me - and now the detection of Myra's medical condition, all within a span of a few months. The timing of the tragic strikes might have been coincidental, but the pattern within them was unmistakable.

The pragmatic side of me however knew that it was Avantika whose sturdy presence had given me the strength to tide over the shower of misfortunes. At least those that I had managed to tide over for now. If it wasn't for her, I might not have taken up the job I did or even settled for the small flat we were presently living in.

'What other options did I have?' you might ask.

My state was no less than that of a warrior in the midst of battle, faced with an all-powerful adversary. I had the choice of holding my ground and perishing right where I stood or to step back, lose some ground, and wait for an opportunity to strike back. The second was obviously more rational among the options, but combatants, when left to their own, are seldom known to bring themselves to opt for a retreat. Their pride, the surge of blood in their veins and the lure of martyrdom often stands in their way. I too, I had a feeling, would have gone down battling my fate had it not been for Avantika.

When the results of Myra's tests came, Avantika was once again there with me, indulgently rebutting the dreadful things I had read about aplastic anaemia on the Internet. 'Nothing can happen to Myra. She will be fine soon, you shall see. But you need to get a grip over yourself… If you continue moving about with a morose face like that, you would only be doing her more harm than good,' she would say.

And rightly enough, the medicines that Myra was being made to endlessly pop brought some good with them, as the symptoms – the headaches and the dizziness – were soon a thing of the past. In about a week, Myra had regained her vitality and not only did she resume school, but she also began befriending other kids, apparently adjusting with the situation she found herself in the midst of. Little did I know then that this was just a momentary reprieve, a breather of sorts, which my hostile fate had mercifully extended before dealing the more severe blows!

In less than a month's time, Myra's aches had returned and with a renewed vigour now. They were significantly severe in their new avatar, impaling her to an extent which prohibited her from attending school and going about her usual chores. The medicines too, after the initial taste of success, seemed to have bowed down to the relentlessness of her ailment and once again we found ourselves doing rounds of the doctor's clinic. It was a painful experience, especially the derived agony I had to endure as a consequence of Myra's suffering, and the days when Avantika was not around, I would miss her terribly.

I can't say if I was being selfish, perhaps I was, but what else was a drowning man to do but latch on to anything his hands brushed against? Avantika had claimed a place in our lives at her own accord, uninvited and unprompted, and now when she had become a necessity of sorts, I was but entitled to my fair share of expectations. Of course I hadn't taken the trouble of slotting her in one of the neo-societal relationship compartments and neither had I reflected upon my fitment into her scheme of things. But then, with the goings-on in my own life, I was barely left with any mind space to devote to such banalities.

A month went by and then another, but despite changing two doctors, subjecting Myra to several tests and switching her medication many times, her condition simply refused to improve. She had become frail, refusing to eat even her favourite foods, and the circles around her eyes were continually growing darker. She had been able to attend school only three out of the past fifteen weekdays, feeling too weak to move out of the house on most mornings. Worry had become a permanent occupant in my mind and my efforts to put up a brave face for Myra - venting my agony in the form of tears in the quiet of the night, and come morning, acting as though things were just the way they were meant to be - had begun waning too.

I had become excessively irate, snapping at the slightest of pretexts and doling out mouthfuls to anyone within an earshot. The daytime house-help, Avantika and on a couple of occasions even Arden had to face the brunt of my temper. It was nothing short of a miracle that none of them ever chose to retaliate.

'Mr. Singh, there is something I needed to discuss with you,' said Myra's latest doctor, a renowned super-specialist from one of the famous hospitals in the city. This was our third consultation visit and his prescription too, like that of his predecessors, was failing to have the desired effect.

I nodded gravely.

'I have reviewed the patient's medical history and going by the absence of any favourable response to oral medication, I believe it is time we should consider the option of bone marrow transplant,' he began. I had done enough research on the subject to know that this was the last resort for doctors when it came to treating patients suffering from aplastic anaemia. Having an expert recommend it for my own daughter was like being hit by a bolt of lightning. I sat there gaping at him, numbness spreading across my limbs.

'You are of course free to seek a second opinion, but in my view it is time we looked at that option for Myra. Presently we can look at an autologous transplant, extracting her own marrow and administering it back after treating it, but if we delay this further, we might be faced with the added challenge of getting a matching donor for her.'

Avantika's grip tightened around my hand as she heard this. She had landed up in Mumbai only the last evening, further fuelling my suspicion that it wasn't by pure chance that she often showed up around the time that Myra had to be taken to the hospital. Myra, on the doctor's instructions, was waiting in the antechamber while Avantika and I sat across his desk, listening frightfully to his opinion. I turned to glance at her but her eyes were affixed on the doctor as though she were expecting him to utter a further set of words that would somehow negate what he had just said.

'But Myra is just a small child and the procedure, I am sure, will be extremely taxing for her. Isn't there any other option that we could look at?' I shot back after a brief pause. There was more than a tinge of desperation in my voice and the doctor seemed conscious of it.

'It will be strenuous alright, especially the part where we destroy her existing marrow and condition her body to accept the transplanted tissues. The radiation therapy used for this will not be easy on Myra... The marrow harvesting and the transplantation itself are, however, much simpler processes and take about an hour each. We can use intravenous sedatives and she will not even feel a pinch... Given her age, I myself wanted to avoid a transplant to the extent possible, but I am afraid, there is no other alternative we are left with. The silver lining though is that having age by her side will help her recover faster and the chances of the procedure being able to cure the ailment permanently are also significantly high.'

For the next fifteen minutes or so we persistently quizzed the doctor on the bone marrow transplant procedure, likelihood of its success and the possible ramifications and after-effects. Much to our horror, we learnt that Myra would have to undergo chemotherapy for destroying the dysfunctional marrow within her, once the harvesting was done. Chemotherapy wasn't an alien term for either Avantika or me. We had heard and seen enough of it to know that it was used for the treatment of cancer and more often than not left the patients suffering from severe hair loss and fatigue, making them resemble a human skeleton of sorts. The revelation nearly froze my spine stiff.

That wasn't all. Myra, during the phase of post-transplant recovery, might also be required to undergo several rounds of blood transfusion. The doctor, despite his attempts to sound reassuring, came across as a heartless monster who was unhesitatingly proposing to drain and replace the vital fluids flowing within the body of an innocent little girl. But we were aware that he was an expert in his field and no other haematologist in the country would dare contradict his recommendations.

'How much is the procedure like to cost?' I asked eventually.

'That is a function of how she responds to the treatment and how many days she has to remain in the hospital. However, it could range from 15 to 25 lakh rupees.'

My reaction would have shown on my face for that was when Avantika turned to look at me. The figure had obviously left me flustered. On another day, a few years back in time, it wouldn't have taken much for me to put together the amount but today it sounded like someone was asking me to scale the Mount Everest barefoot. My previous employers had a medical insurance policy for their employees and kin, which would have covered a fraction of Myra's treatment cost. But now even that tiny bit of support was gone.

Not a word was spoken between Avantika and me on our way back. Perhaps it was Myra's presence in the taxi that prevented a dialogue or maybe Avantika understood the precarious position I was in, but I was glad for the quiet nevertheless. Myra was too weak to talk and, resting her head in Avantika Aunty's lap, had gone off to sleep on the back seat.

'Is it the money?' she enquired once we were home and Myra had been tucked into bed.

'What do you mean, 'is it the money'? The money can be arranged, but what about Myra. How will she endure chemotherapy and God knows how many rounds of blood transfusion? Do you even have an idea what that means?' I screamed out. My outburst was a result of my own frustrations as well as the fact that Avantika had so effortlessly managed to pinpoint its root cause. My haplessness was personal and I had no intentions of making it public.

'But there isn't another option, is there? She will go through hell, I concede, but that will be for just the one time. And it will forever rid her of the pain she has to endure on an everyday basis. Rahul, you need to think from your mind and not your heart. The transplant is critical for Myra and the sooner we are able to get it done, the better it will be for her,' she counselled.

Despite the consideration in her tone I argued for a while, just for the heck of it, before acknowledging her words. I had known even while exiting from the doctor's chamber that the transfusion was a must but the question gripping me was how I was going to raise the needed funds.

We sat in the drawing room, chatting, sharing our grief and sorrows for a long time and when words began to run short, Avantika got up and headed for the bedroom to join Myra. I reached out for the folded mattress and began laying it out on the floor for my own use when I heard her call out my name.

I looked up. Avantika was holding the bedroom door ajar with one hand, ready to step in, her head cocked over her shoulders to look at me. 'In case the money does become a concern, please do let me know. I have some savings that we could use to cover the medical expenses. The money is lying idle in the bank and I have no immediate use for it. You can of course return it to me later,' she said. I knew that my bluff had been called in the very first hand and there was no point in persisting with it, so I responded with a quiet nod. She smiled back, a faint compassionate stretch of the lips, before dissolving into the darkness beyond the open door.

Avantika had ever so casually offered to eliminate the immediate obstacle in my path, but I couldn't allow her to expend her life's savings for the sake my daughter. Call it vanity or arrogance, but I wasn't prepared to become a parasite just as yet. Avantika had done enough for Myra and me already and this one responsibility I wasn't looking to shirk away from.

Next day, Avantika, dressed in her navy blue uniform, left to join her crew in ferrying hundreds of unknown travellers to their destination, with an unstated promise to return soon. She refrained from talking about the money or even Myra's treatment and I avoided bringing up the topic either. Instead, I got down to weighing the sources I could tap for raising the capital I desperately required.

The divorce had flushed me of everything that came remotely close to being termed an asset and between my mutual fund investments and the two savings accounts, my net worth now stood at just under a measly two lakh rupees. I had even sold off my watch; the Omega that Shalini had gifted me for our first anniversary, to cover for Myra's ever-mounting medical expenses. I glanced at the Esprit that now rested on my wrist as a replacement.

It was my thirty-fourth birthday a few months back, a day I had very nearly forgotten until Avantika had suddenly turned up at the door with a bunch of flowers, a cake and a neatly-wrapped packet to remind me of it. The packet contained the watch I was now wearing. She had noticed that my regular watch had gone missing one fine day, and instead of posing questions that might embarrass me, she had opted to remain quiet and buy me a replacement when the occasion permitted her to. How I wished that Shalini had been half as sensitive as Avantika.

Parting with the Omega hadn't pained me to the slightest bit. It was just a normal transaction. I gave away the watch and got the money in return. I thought about what it would be like if I had to sell the Esprit watch as well and I winced impulsively. Not this one! This held much higher sentimental value for me than its opulent cousin that I had previously owned.

The fact however was that even if I shoved my emotions aside and took the watch to the pawn shop, it wouldn't make the slightest dent in the astronomical sum of money I needed. I, therefore, decided to return my thoughts to the immediate task at hand, figuring the avenues I could tap to come up with the money.

My contribution till date to Arden's business was a glaring naught and that didn't leave me with much face to seek an advance from him. Moreover, in my professional capacity, I was privy to the business financials and I knew that Arden, as much as he might have wanted to, was not in a position to release the kind of funds I needed.

Over the next couple of days I visited both banks I had entrusted my accounts with and filled out personal loan application forms. It was strange, I mused, that when I did not require a loan, pesky tele-callers wouldn't stop ringing me at the oddest hours of the day offering loans for or against anything that could be tagged with a price. And now, when the need was indeed grave, I had somehow managed to fall off their radar. I couldn't recall having heard from them over the past several months. Hell, no one had even tried to sell me a holiday club membership or a credit card lately. My life was indeed spiralling bottomward and rapidly gaining momentum as it did so.

After an assurance from the enthusiastic loan officer that I would hear from him within the next three working days, I returned to office, harbouring a rare streak of optimism. When you have been pushed to the darkest corners of existence, even a bleak glimmer of light appears like a blinding eruption of candescence. My state was no different.

Myra had been feeling better that morning, good enough to get ready and head to school. And with my loan application under process, I had a feeling that the situation would once again surrender its reins to me shortly. I would have to make room for the instalments in my already pruned wages but we would nevertheless manage to keep afloat.

The optimism had persisted till I reached home that evening, and the sight of Myra engrossed in her favourite cartoon show helped it soar further. The maid, whose day-end was a function of my return from work, eagerly handed back Myra's custody and made for the door. 'Saheb, a letter came in for you this afternoon. I have left it here,' she said, signalling with her hand towards the mantelpiece before stepping out. I nodded without making any efforts to get up from the sofa. The letter was not running away from where it had been placed and I could always read it a little later.

It was a registered post, and the pre-printed return address on the envelope made the hair at the back of my neck rise and my heart cringe. The letter had originated from the offices of the same law firm that Shalini had engaged to represent her during the divorce proceedings. Gripped with sudden anxiety, I tore it open and unfolded the official-looking document I found inside. The first word to catch my attention, printed in bold on the firm's letterhead was 'N O T I C E'.

Shalini had served me a legal notice disputing the court's grant of Myra's custody to me. The reason, the notice stated, was that I was financially incapable of taking care of my daughter's needs.

I continued reading, my teeth clenched hard and my hands trembling with fury. The notice mentioned, right up to last detail, my sacking from the organisation I was previously employed with and the 'unstable' job I was currently pursuing. To my utter amazement it even cited details of Myra's medical condition and the estimated cost for her treatment, a fact that Shalini had no straightforward way of knowing. Since neither my income and nor my savings were enough to take care of Myra's treatment and her upkeep, the notice alleged, I should reassign her custody to Shalini. There was a date by which I was expected to respond to the notice, failing which the law firm had threatened to take the matter to a higher court.

'The Bitch,' I muttered under my breath. We had just finished dinner and Myra had retired to her room. But it would be some time before she fell asleep and till she did that I had to avoid speaking aloud my reactions. Still clutching the document, I slumped back on the sofa and began reflecting over what I had read.

Shalini was bound to know about my dismissal from the job, she was responsible for orchestrating it after all, but how did she know about where I was working now? And about Myra's condition, how was it ever possible that Shalini knew not only the details of the disorder, but also the proposed treatment and its estimated cost?

There was something gravely wrong somewhere. Both Myra's doctor and the hospital she was being treated in had a reputation to protect and neither would commit the blunder of parting with confidential information about one of their patients just like that. There certainly was more to it than met the eye.

Had Shalini engaged someone to keep an eye on me, a detective agency perhaps?

The thought was most disconcerting and suddenly I began to remember (and conjure up) instances where I had felt like I was being watched. A stranger on the road whose eyes had met mine and remained locked for a flicker too long, the security guard at the office who had been looking at me somewhat keenly of late, the auto driver who had driven me home and seemed hell bent upon striking conversation, suddenly it seemed to me as if half the city of Mumbai was on Shalini's payrolls.

I realised that my overzealous imagination was playing havoc within my head but it was all very spooky nonetheless. So instead of worrying about Shalini's faceless informants I consciously shifted my attention to the contents of the notice.

Shalini had chosen to strike when the proverbial iron was smouldering. She would have known that I would arrange for the funds needed for Myra's treatment come what may, but the cost of another extended courtroom battle would prove my undoing and that was precisely the weakness she intended to exploit. This bit was understandable. Both of us wanted Myra's custody and it was only fair that she was attempting to seize the one opportunity she saw. I would have done the same. I too wouldn't have stopped at anything to prevent Myra from being taken away from me and neither was I going to.

What left me disgusted though was that she chose to use Myra's condition as a tool to further her interests, indifferent to the pain and agony the little girl was enduring. She was a mother and when she learnt about her own daughter's state, what stopped Shalini from rushing to Mumbai to be by her side? Whether Myra accepted it or not, she needed her mother the most at this time and Shalini, instead, had opted to stay back in Delhi and manipulate the situation to her advantage. I was appalled to even think that she was the same girl I had once fallen in love with and had vowed to take care of for the rest of her living years.

Firming up my mind about what needed to be done, I went to the bedroom to check on Myra. She was sound asleep by now. Shutting the door behind me, I returned to the drawing room and dialled a number on my mobile phone.

'Hello,' the brusque voice of Shalini's father greeted me.

'It is Rahul this side. I need to have a word with Shalini…,' I returned, blending courtesy and bluntness in just the right proportion.

There was a brief pause which sounded like a thousand snakes hissing in unison. 'Of course,' he said, breaking the silence finally. I heard him call out Shalini's name followed by a ruffle and a slight whispering noise. It was as if he had covered the mouthpiece to pass on a hurried set of instructions to his daughter before she was exposed to me.

'Hello,' I finally heard her voice. It was colder than an icicle.

We had met in the courtroom during the divorce proceedings, heard each other speak, but refrained from addressing one another directly. This was the first one-on-one conversation we were having since the morning Shalini had walked out of the house. But strangely her voice didn't result in any nostalgia, any craving to return to the times gone by for me. She sounded distant and aloof and I was only too happy to let her remain that way.

'I wanted to talk to you about the notice your lawyers have sent,' I stated without indulging in a more eloquent opening.

'Tell me,' she returned just as crustily. Once again I was disappointed in her. Maybe some part of me was still hoping that the first thing she would enquire about was Myra and her health.

'You can get your father have me kicked out of my job or do whatever else you like but get one thing straight, nothing is going to let you snatch my daughter away from me.' My annoyance distorted my words to make them sound very different from what I had originally intended.

'Oh yes? And I should let her remain with you so that you can get her the cheapest bargain for her treatment? Accept it Rahul, you have lost the plot. You are not capable of taking care of your daughter anymore and it is in her interest that I want you to return her to me,' she said. She had begun by matching the agitation in my voice but surprisingly she checked it midway and switched to a consultative tone instead. This deliberate composure of hers ended up peeving me beyond words.

'I am more than capable of taking care of Myra and it is entirely my business how and where I get her treated, not yours,' I nearly screamed. 'And why don't you speak for yourself? What kind of a mother are you that even after learning about your daughter's illness you have no desire of seeing her? Instead you are busy scheming with your lawyers about how you can use the situation to get back at me. You are nothing but a cold-blooded manipulator, just like your father, only this time you have faltered in choosing your adversary. No matter what levels you stoop to or what Machiavellian ways you resort to, Myra is going nowhere.'

'Don't even dare to utter another word about my father! What gives you the right to lecture me when you are yourself busy frolicking with that new mistress of yours right under your ailing daughter's nose? Don't be under the impression that you will ever be able to get that whore to take my place. Myra is my daughter and I will get her custody no matter what it takes,' she shot back.

The tremble in her voice was unmistakable. She was angry, terribly angry. But I was furious too. She knew about Avantika as well. What the hell had she been up to?

'I should have known better than to expect you to play fair. What you have now hired snoops to tail me, is it? Do what you may but you are going to face bitter defeat once again, there is no preventing that. As for Avantika, she is nothing like you. She loves Myra in a manner that you were never capable of and your own daughter will vouch for that. Just like she chose to stay with me instead of you the last time,' I replied, using words that were likely to sting her hard. And if her retort was anything to go by, I had succeeded.

'You tutored Myra into saying what she did in front of the judge. Else there was no way she would have chosen you over me. And as for that whore, she stays in Delhi only right? Let her even try to take my place in my daughter's life and I shall show her who she is messing around with. She has no idea what she is getting into, but she will soon find that out the hard way,' she growled.

We were both spewing venom by the litre and the discussion was heading nowhere in particular. So, after letting out some more steam I disconnected the call abruptly. I had called Shalini intending to assure her that Myra will get the best treatment possible and convince her to retract the notice. But clearly, I had raised my hopes beyond the realms of actuality and the only contentment I could take away from the conversation was that of getting the last word in, deviously of course. The notice had to be given a befitting rejoinder and I still had to figure out how I was going to manage that.

There were seven missed calls on my phone when I disconnected Shalini's call. All of them from the same number, Avantika's!

It had become a ritual of sorts between us. Whenever she was not in Mumbai, she would call every evening to check on Myra's health and I would apprise her of the day's happenings, whatever little things there were to share. These conversations had acquired a therapeutic character as I felt lighter after having spoken to her, as if a load had lifted from my chest. But not today! I was in no state to strike a conversation now and so I chose to send her a text message instead. I informed her that all was well with Myra and that I would call her the next morning since I had hit the bed already and was very nearly asleep.

I did call Avantika the next morning, but I refrained from mentioning my conversation with Shalini from the previous evening. Now that my mind was adequately rested, I felt silly about some of the things I had said and the manner in which I had gone about the conversation in general. Moreover, what could I tell Avantika, that Shalini thought she was a whore? Or that she had threatened to harm her if she tried getting close to Myra?

I told her about the notice and Avantika was alarmed on hearing of its contents.

'This is serious. We will need to respond to the notice. Anyway, I will be in Mumbai the day after tomorrow and let us talk through it then. Meanwhile, don't fret yourself much over it and focus on Myra and her health instead,' she suggested.

It was easier said than done. The conversation with Shalini remained with me through the day, intermittently showing up as a distended tendon, clenched fists or gritting teeth, as I recalled the toxicity of her words. Sometime around the evening a telephone call managed to divert my attention away from it. The caller was my relationship manager at one of the banks.

'Sir, I have received the approval for your loan application and you can come tomorrow to complete the disbursement formalities,' he began, a wave of relief gushing through me as a consequence of what he said. But in less than a split-second the relief had transformed into a feeling of unqualified fear. 'However, there is one slight glitch. The credit team, after carefully appraising your application, has sanctioned an unsecured loan of only Rs 3lakh. So, to avail a loan of the entire Rs 15 lakh that you have applied for, you will need to provide a security of the same value. Anything, a fixed deposit or a mutual fund investment…' he said, allowing his words to tail.

'If I had a fixed deposit for the amount I need, why on earth would I ask you guys for a loan?' I reasoned.

'I understand Sir, but we are open to accepting any type of asset as collateral, a property that you have in your name or even gold for that matter. No other bank will offer you such flexibility.'

I reasoned with him some more but in utter futility. He was an insignificant cog in the wheel and was only conveying a decision that had already been made by the intellectuals in their back offices, attempting to make it sound as inoffensive as he could. Of course the salesman in him was hopeful that he could still close a sale by offering me another product, a secured loan, where the collateral being pledged to the bank served as a basis for the loan and not the credit-worthiness of the borrower. How could I tell him that I had nothing to offer him, not a piece of property and certainly not pots of gold?

When I disconnected the call, my knuckles were white and my fingers felt as if I had left them in the refrigerator for a while. This was completely unexpected. When I had applied for the loan, the possibility that I might no longer be worthy of it had neither occurred to me and nor had the officer indicated anything of the sort. Just to be sure, I had applied for loans with two banks and was certain that at least one of them would take care of my immediate concern. In fact, it was this surety that had reflected as confidence in my voice during my conversation with Shalini the other day. And now, the confidence was rapidly waning.

The credit appraisal process for most banks, I knew, followed a similar pattern. And if one of them had decided that I wasn't worth taking a risk with their money, there was only a slim chance that the other would think otherwise. It was a little late to call up the officer of the second bank, so I decided to pay him a visit the next morning. Though my mind already knew the outcome of the visit, my hopeful heart refused to play along. In less than fifteen hours, my mind had claimed a resounding victory over my heart.

Once again the tiny glimmer of hope I had been using as a guiding light was mercilessly extinguished and once again I was grappling in the dark, my hands flailing in search of a support.

Avantika arrived around nine o'clock the next morning. She was on an early morning Mumbai – Delhi flight and was slated to return the next morning. I must have presented a real awful sight as the first words she spoke upon setting her eyes on me were, 'What on earth has happened to you?'

Well, my eyes were bloodshot and puffy from the lack of sleep the previous night, but I left that for her to decipher.

'Nothing, I am fine,' I said instead.

But Avantika wasn't one to give up so easily. She retreated then, only to return once she had changed her clothes and spent some time chatting with Myra, about forty minutes or so in all. She was relentless and it was only after I had informed her of my faring with the banks that she stood down.

'Rahul, you are not to be blamed for your condition. You had a soaring career and enough assets to show for it as well, but what were you to do if someone you thought to be your own betrayed you and took it all away? There is no stopping you from achieving the heights you have already once scaled, only the present situation needs to be negotiated somehow…'

I knew where she was heading with her dialogue, but I chose to remain silent.

'I don't mean to bruise your ego or hurt your pride, but isn't it only logical that we use my money for Myra's treatment? It is anyway lying idle in the bank. You can return it to me when you are in a position to. Plus, you have the notice to take care of… Remember? How do you propose to do that if you remain preoccupied thinking of ways to raise the money? Listen to me for once,' she nearly pleaded.

I still couldn't brush aside my reluctance to accept Avantika's money but, I must confess, the thought had pervaded my mind a couple of times during the preceding night. I had been thinking of avenues to raise the money but nothing concrete was showing up, and then, Avantika's face and her words from the past came to me. 'I have the money,' wasn't that what she had said?

Who knew, if nothing else worked out, I might actually be compelled to consider her offer, steamrolling over my pride, vanity, ego and other such. So, instead of contradicting her, I opted to push the matter under the proverbial carpet for the time being. 'Let's see. We will take a call on that when we have to,' I said, adding a thoughtful nod for effect.

Avantika didn't persist, sensitive perhaps to my views on the matter, and returned to the room where Myra was asleep.

The day continued progressing at a painfully slow pace like it usually does in those phases when one is left with nothing to look forward to from the days to follow. There was no silver lining in the dark clouds casting a shadow over my life and I could only sit and rue the evil designs of my fate. I was doing just that, sitting on the sofa and trying to answer the ever so difficult question, why me, when the ever-elusive sleep quietly approached and consumed me.

It was sometime in the night – I can't recall the exact reading on the wall clock. Myra had gone to bed, put to sleep by Avantika.

When Avantika was staying with us she and Myra would share the bedroom while I would be forced to make do with a make-shift bed on the floor of the hall. It was in the hall that I was sitting pensively, clutching a glass brimming with rum and cola.

'You know Rahul; life is too beautiful to be drowned in sorrows. You must get a grip on yourself and put a brave face, If not for your own self, then for Myra. And for me,' she said. She was still nursing her first drink whereas I was on my fourth, or was it the fifth, I couldn't recall. She had placed her hand over mine and broken the prevailing silence with her words. I could only nod in return.

'I don't know about you, but Myra and you mean the world to me and it pains me immensely to see you like this,' she added. I was amazed at the effortlessness of her statement. She had simply, as a matter of fact, stated something that a part of me had been aching to hear but never had the courage to seek out. I looked up, into her eyes and saw a maze of emotions that left little doubt that she meant every word that she had spoken. Instinctively, I reached out and hugged her. She reciprocated by wrapping her arms around me, and we remained like that, frozen in the moment, for what seemed like eternity.

Then abruptly she withdrew and rushed back to the bedroom. I called out her name, whispered actually, for the fear of disturbing Myra's sleep, but she did not turn back and I did not pursue her. She had mustered the courage to speak her heart out and if she needed some time alone to come to terms with it, I had no business denying her that.

My woes hadn't subsided, neither had I found a magic wand to rid me of my difficulties, but with our expression of love, albeit nebulous, my heart had begun soaring into a hemisphere it had hitherto forgotten. As I thought about Avantika, breaching dimensions that had remained unexplored and untouched in my mind, partly because of my preoccupations and partly due to the fear of taking the initiative – she was a successful single girl and I a divorced father after all – I felt a calmness of purpose settle somewhere deep inside me. That night, following many a sleepless ones, I slept in peace, pleasuring from the unrestrained fantasies my throbbing heart was busy conjuring.

I could feel it, love was once again forcing its way into my life and I was greeting it with open arms. I wasn't sure if I was prepared for it, but then, who is ever prepared for love?

The next morning Avantika left, casually, as she always did, and carefree, as if our conversation from the previous night was merely a figment of my imagination and had never actually played out in real. But she was like that, always in control and never susceptible or unguarded. She had probably gone to sleep cursing herself for allowing her emotions to show and by the morning she was sure to have plugged the accidental fissure to perfection. But the damage had been done. I had caught a glimpse of her innermost feelings and a time would come when she would have no option but to acknowledge them.

Only if I had some way of knowing that in two weeks from then I would find myself in Delhi endeavouring to locate a missing Avantika. Had I known so, I could have tried to get her to confess her love for me before she left. Or I could at least have shared my own feelings and told her some of the many things I had mulled over that night. But as the saying goes, 'If wishes were horses, beggars would ride.'

Ten

Anand listened to the entire account patiently, as if I were sharing some spicy bit of tinsel town gossip. I had spoken uninterruptedly for nearly forty minutes, giving him a condensed view of the past few years of my life, elaborating slightly when treading on the more pertinent sections – Shalini's intimidating threat and Avantika's subsequent disappearance.

He pushed a glass of water towards me and as I tended to my parched throat, he spoke. 'What about Myra's treatment then? Have you managed to raise the money yet?'

I should have been touched by his concern but, instead, I was peeved. Unknowingly he had pricked the sore spot I had been desperately avoiding, even in my thoughts.

'Yes, I have spoken to a few people. Something should come up soon,' I said, trying not to sound too curt.

It wasn't a lie. I had indeed spoken to people, Arden for instance, and had even applied for loans with every other financial institution engaged in the business of retail lending. The guy at one of the NBFCs had even guaranteed that my application would get approved. But in this world of documentation and evidence, what weight did a verbal assurance hold?

Despite my best efforts, I wasn't sure of being entertained at any of the doors I had knocked and thus I had chosen the easy way out: not think about what I couldn't control and focus instead on looking for Avantika. Now that Anand had accidently unveiled the nuisance, I could feel myself palpitating and my pulse racing madly as the fear of not being able to fend for Myra began gripping me once again.

'As for Shalini's threat, I don't think that is ground enough for us to talk to her. We will need to start afresh with the search,' Anand's words veered me back from the clutches of my fearful thoughts. He seemed to be thinking out aloud rather than addressing me.

'Why can't you question her? You are the police, and she did threaten to 'show Avantika who she was messing with'. I am a witness to that dialogue,' I interjected.

'Yes, but she was angry then, you guys were having an argument. People say lots of things when they are angry and mostly they don't mean any of them… In fact I am reasonably certain that Shalini wouldn't have anything to do with this.'

'How can you be so certain? You don't know what she is capable of… She will stop at nothing to have her way. And her father, the lesser said about him the better,' I reasoned.

'Call it a cop's intuition but I am sure that Shalini is not behind this. Had it been any other girl I would have taken a chance and spoken to her, even if it served no purpose other than curbing your curiosity. Middle class folks usually get hassled just by the sight of a policeman knocking on their doors. It is easy to command their cooperation as they are too harried and scared to question our actions, but not someone like Shalini's father. He will shred us apart if we land up at his doorstep without a satisfactory reason. Who knows, he might use his clout to get me suspended even,' Anand replied.

I wasn't entirely convinced about his intuition, it was I who was once married to Shalini and not him, but everything else he said made sense. There was no point in persisting with the debate. I couldn't possibly ask him to risk his job for the sake of interrogating Shalini. And even if I was stubborn and senseless enough to do so, I had little doubt that he would refuse.

'Where do you intend to begin in that case?' I asked instead.

'Let me mull this over and figure out the angles we should start exploring. I will call you as soon as something comes up. You don't have anything else planned for tomorrow, do you?'

Assuring him of my availability, I took Anand's leave and hailed an auto-rickshaw for the hotel that Tiwari, the watchman, had recommended. Anand had enquired about my destination and offered to drop me but I had been quick to turn him down. Nothing about my situation was hidden from him but even then I could not bring myself to tell him that I would be staying in a Rs 450 a night hotel. I was tumbling down the social ladder but I still hadn't lost the sense to conceal my fall.

One look at the hotel and I was glad that I hadn't permitted Anand to accompany me. The hotel, if you must call it that, comprised the second floor of a dilapidated building somewhere along the circuitous alleys of Munirka Village. There was a small painted board proclaiming its existence and had it not been for the helpful paan-wallah we had sought directions from, there was no way I would have noticed it, the ensuing darkness notwithstanding.

After I had paid the rent in advance, the brusque receptionist-cum-porter-cum-manager showed me to my room. That was the good thing about such places, no need for reservations. You could simply land up, ask for a room and get it. No unwarranted questions, no documentation, nothing. If by some stroke of misfortune a room wasn't available, a top-up of 50 rupees would ensure that one materialised instantly.

I had seen many such places thriving in the narrow and busy lanes of Pune, Mumbai and the numerous other cities I had travelled to in the past. No matter where you went, the character of such places remained indistinct. They were like a bunch of cousins, many thousands of them, who had spread to the dingy and dark by lanes of any city that attracted visitors, clandestine or otherwise.

The room, lit by a lone bulb, was damp and a putrid smell hung in the air. The furnishing consisted of a gaudy curtain, a bed with sheets that could well have been slept in by one of Akbar's concubines in their better days and a side table with several scratches and abrasions. The fan, as my escort pressed a switch, came to life with a guttural noise as if resisting the call for getting into action. It was just like I had expected it to be – shoddy and decrepit. In fact if the room had turned out to be anything else, a little more habitable maybe, I might have been disappointed.

Bolting the door behind me, I dumped my overnighter on the side table and dropped myself on the bed. I was sapped, not having the energy needed to change or even to check out the excuse of an attached bathroom. Soon I was drifting into a world within my head, the world of my thoughts, my immediate surroundings reduced to a blurry watermark.

Why was I here, looking for Avantika, when I should have been in Mumbai trying to arrange for the money I required for Myra's treatment? Maybe because she was the only certain source left who could lend me the money? I needed to find her, anyhow, somehow, for Myra's sake.

Wait! Was it all about the money? Had I stooped so low, dragged by my deteriorating situation, that money had become the end for me? Would I not have come to Delhi had it not been for the money? I might have. I would have. After all, Avantika had been with me through my thick and thin, guiding me, helping me and giving me the confidence to battle on.

But why had she done that? She was pretty, had a decent career ahead of her, she could have found anyone, an eligible good-looking bachelor to shower her affection upon. Why then did she choose a divorced man with a daughter over the others?

Maybe it wasn't me and it was Myra. But why even Myra? She is a sweet child and she means the world to me, but then I am her father. She is meant to mean the world to me. What is she to Avantika? There will come a day that Avantika will have her own kids and she can shower them with all the love and affection she wants, why Myra then?

The questions were many and the answers few. For the first time, in this dingy hotel room, I had found the time to reflect upon Avantika's presence in my life. The more I thought about it, the more confusion I found myself grappling with. There was just the solitary piece that appeared to fit in the jigsaw perfectly, that by some quirk of fate she had fallen in love with me. Didn't they proclaim love to be blind? Maybe she hadn't seen what she was getting into and when she did, it might have been too late.

She loved me alright but did I feel the same way about her or was she simply a matter of convenience for me? Someone I could uninhibitedly share my woes with and get the load off my back, momentarily albeit.

I thought about her, fighting a sudden surge of guilt at having ignored her feelings all along, at having taken her for granted. I felt a twinge in my stomach and I tried to assuage it by justifying my actions to my own conscious.

When did I have the time to think about love? It was all happening so fast. My life was crumbling all around me and it was only fair that in my desperate attempts to resurrect it, I missed giving Avantika her due. But I did love her. Why else would I long to speak to her every evening? Why would I look forward to her next visit within hours of her departure from my house? What was it that had made me accept her as a part of my family, letting her sleep in the room with Myra while I slept on the floor? If this wasn't love, what was?

And what was it that I had felt when she had embraced me on the night before her disappearance? I had felt as if all my worries were melting in the heat of her embrace. I had felt much lighter, ready to take on anything that destiny decided to hurl my way. Her touch, there was nothing sensual about it, just a warm cuddle that had the wherewithal to metamorphose two souls into one.

After Shalini, I had begun to doubt the very existence of love. I wasn't sure if human bonds, the eternal variety, could be forged outside the natural linkages of blood. But Avantika, with her selflessness and devotion, had once again turned me into a believer. I could now say with certainty that love existed and that I was in love with her. Yes, I was indeed in love with Avantika. The thought made my lips curl into a brief smile, but anguish was quick to recover its lost ground.

Where was she? What was she doing at that moment? What kind of trouble was she in which prevented her from contacting me? Involuntarily, I reached out for my phone and checked if it was on. It was, and there was no missed call or message from Avantika.

Then suddenly I remembered something. Shalini!

It had never occurred to me that Shalini might have a hand in Avantika's disappearance but Anand's question had compelled me to consider the possibility. And once I had done that, I was very nearly convinced that she was the one responsible for it. Of course Anand had rubbished the theory, some of his arguments making sense even, but I was not entirely convinced about Shalini's innocence.

Hadn't she gone to the extent of finding out about Avantika, through who knows what dubious means? What business did she have doing that when the two of us were already divorced? Anand didn't know Shalini, I did. She and that father of hers, blinded by power and money, were capable of many things that we common-folk would not even dare to imagine. She might not be a prime suspect alright, but she was still an avenue worth exploring. If Anand, constrained by the lack of concrete evidence, found his hands tied, I was still free to make enquiries of my own.

My phone was already in my hand. I checked the time. It was 10.40 p.m. Not too late by big-city standards. I could still make the call. I scrolled down my contacts-list and pressed the green button upon reaching the entry, 'Shalini Residence'.

After three rings I heard a male voice on the line. It was the servant. I introduced myself and asked for Shalini.

'One moment,' he said, leaving me to contend with the innocuous sound of static intermingled with traces of a whispered exchange. He was back in no time, to inform me that Shalini was already asleep and could not attend the call. The man was a slave to the instructions he received and there was no point arguing with him. After my last conversation with Shalini, I had once again been estranged, even in the remote world of telephony, and I had no option but to disconnect the call.

I was frustrated at not being able to question Shalini about Avantika and my thoughts were soon veering into a more ominous sphere. What if Shalini had indeed got someone to 'take care' of Avantika? What if Avantika was dead already? Was that why Shalini had refused to talk to me? She would have known that her voice would betray her guilt even if her words did not. My heart was once again thumping madly, as if a professional boxer was using it for sparring practice, and I had to struggle hard to suppress my fears and slip into much needed slumber.

The sun was up already when I got up the next morning. Its rays, brutal and excruciating, were flowing in from the window and bathing me entirely. The curtain, a feeble stretch of plastic, was still in its place, but clearly, in the many years of hanging undisturbed, it had forgotten the very purpose that it was set to serve. Wincing my eyes, I got up and made for the bathroom – a unit about which the lesser we speak, the better.

I took my time in freshening up and once done I looked around for the intercom – I had skipped dinner and was already feeling like my interiors had turned into one big hollow – there wasn't anything resembling a telephone instrument in the room. Pulling the door ajar, I peered in the direction of the reception. The same man from last night was sitting there, no evidence visible of him having moved from the seat after showing me to the room last night. I approached the desk and asked him the options for breakfast. He looked at me as if I had asked him the coordinates for Pakistan's nuclear bases instead.

The hotel did not serve food! How silly of me. Wasn't that obvious? In five minutes I was down, scanning the streets of Munirka Village for a decent place that could satisfy my hunger while meeting some basic qualifiers of hygiene.

Having settled for a plate of greasy choley bhature from a rundown kiosk, I was returning to the hotel when my cellphone beeped. The caller was Anand.

'I will be going to inspect Avantika's flat in about half an hour. Would you want to come along?'

Hell yes, I wanted to! I would have preferred being confined to a chamber of the Tihar Jail than the excuse of a room I had spent the night in. In twenty minutes flat, my overnighter dangling securely from my shoulder, I was once again at the Munirka Vihar gate.

'Good morning Sir,' Tiwari greeted me cheerfully. I responded with a nod and a lame smile. 'Hope you found the hotel easily? Was the room okay?'

The job of a security guard can get extremely lonely and mundane, I knew, but I was in no mood to satisfy Tiwari's craving for casual banter. 'Yes, it was fine. Has the Inspector arrived already?' I returned rather brusquely. I had just demoted Anand by a few ranks, but I wasn't sure if Tiwari could differentiate between an Inspector and an Assistant Commissioner of Police. For all you know, a mention of the correct designation might have provided him with more fodder to elongate the conversation.

'No, I haven't seen a policeman all morning. Why, is one expected to visit?' he was persistent in his quest for a dialogue.

'Mr. Sharma, is he here?' I enquired, ignoring his question.

'Yes, Mr. Sharma came in about ten minutes back. He must be at the flat, D-203.'

I was about to head inside and make for the flat when an SUV, marked with the Delhi Police insignia stopped a few metres behind me and Anand stepped out. On his heels were three constables, one woman and two men.

Anand greeted me eagerly, once again recording his displeasure with the fact that I had not agreed to put up with him for the night, before asking me lead him to 'the' flat. He didn't bother to acknowledge Tiwari's stiff salute and marched in as if he were a monarch visiting his stables for an inspection. I could see a sense of awe in Tiwari's eyes, and in Anand's shadow, even I had become a beneficiary of it. The manner in which Anand met me had elevated me in the eyes of the watchman from a nobody to somebody.

I was amazed that I had bothered to take note of Tiwari's reaction and even felt pleased about it. Just where was my life heading, that the admiration of a watchman had begun to matter so much? In another day and age, I would have remained oblivious even to his existence. Engrossed in my self-piteous brooding, I led the small party to Avantika's flat.

Mr. Sharma, a bespectacled, ageing man with a hairline in the last leg of its recession, was waiting for us outside the gate. Anand would have beckoned him, for Mr. Sharma gave him a vigorous shake of the hand before turning to me. The shake I received was a little gentler.

He opened the door with his set of keys and stepped aside. Anand was the first to step inside and I closely followed. This was my first glimpse of Avantika's world, the world she had kept hidden from me despite having established herself firmly in the one I inhabited.

The hall was sparsely but elegantly furnished with a wicker set comprising a three-seater sofa, two chairs and a centre table. The walls, all but one were painted in cream and adorned with a series of Egyptian papyrus paintings mounted in double-glass frames. The farthest wall had a crinkle texture in maroon, matching perfectly with the upholstery. There was a wall-mounted bookshelf with a collection that spoke about the spiritual inclination of its owner.

As Anand's team surveyed the room, searching every nook and corner for any clue it might hold, I couldn't help myself from being sucked into Avantika's world. Images of her lazing on the sofa, a book in hand, a cup of coffee on the table ahead were flashing before my eyes and I was consumed by an irresistible urge to become one with the images. I wanted to be there when Avantika did all the things I was imagining. I yearned to be a part of her life. I yearned to be a part of her.

We moved to the bedroom next, a small passage from the hall leading to a room just as gracefully done up as the hall itself. A double bed covered by a sheet that lacked even the slightest wrinkle, a side table with a stylish reading lamp, a four-door wardrobe and a wall-mounted television set made up the room's furnishings.

'Is this Myra?' Anand's voice veered me from soaking the sights from Avantika's life. He had picked up a photo frame from the side table and was eyeing it curiously. It was a sketch, a machine-made piece of art you can get from any of the shoping malls these days, of Avantika with Myra and me. We had got it made on Avantika's insistence a couple of months back. I wasn't aware that I would find it adorning her bedside table. Hell, I didn't even know that she had taken it with her.

I nodded.

'She is cute. Thank God she didn't take after you,' Anand replied, unable to resist the opportunity to take a slight jab. He had been relatively serious all morning, explicably, given that he was in uniform and in the company of his subordinates. I smiled in response.

I watched as the lady constable went through the wardrobe, carefully sifting through Avantika's belongings. Several sets of her work uniform, the attire which had been synonymous with her arrival as well as her departure from Mumbai, hung neatly on one side. Also hanging were other garments – her salwar suits, denims, tops and dresses – some of which I recalled from her visits.

Once again I was drawn into Avantika's thoughts, only this time they were emerging from the folds of my memories. Her unrestrained laughter when playing with Myra, the look of concern in her eyes when we discussed Myra's ailment, the passion with which she had gone about making a home out of our new rental accommodation and the warm embrace, the most cherished memory of hers she had left me with.

Just then the phone rang. I extracted mine from my pocket but it wasn't the one responsible for the distraction.

'Hello,' I heard Anand speak into his handset. The conversation was brief and his replies monosyllabic but when he disconnected the call and looked at me there was an unmistakable twinkle in his eyes.

'Come, we need to go somewhere,' he said to me and I followed him meekly, not daring to question his authority. As I stepped out of the room, he turned back and began streaming out orders to his deputies. It took him all of three minutes and soon we were in his vehicle, heading to an unknown destination – the two of us and two constables. One of the constables, a male, had been left behind at Munirka Vihar for a reason I couldn't quite fathom and did not have the courage to enquire about.

'Strange! There was nothing in her flat that could tell us where she might be… not a ticket receipt, not a credit card statement, not any signs of a bag having been packed hurriedly, even her toothbrush and other toiletries were right where they were supposed to be. It was all too perfect to be normal, as if someone was deliberately trying to give us the impression that there was nothing out of the ordinary there,' Anand broke the silence eventually. He wasn't addressing me so I remained quiet. I hadn't anyway been able to comprehend what he was implying.

'Tell me,' he suddenly turned to look at me and said, as though he had read my thoughts. 'A house that you live in, no matter what level of a cleanliness freak you might be; can it ever be in such a perfect state? Not a single garment out of place, not a towel on the bed, not a book pulled out from the shelf, not an open carton of milk in the refrigerator, hell, even the doormats were all placed within an inch of perfection. Does this seem normal to you?'

I thought about what he had said and his words suddenly began to make sense. 'You are right! Everything seemed too perfect to be natural,' I replied.

'Exactly! As if somebody, while clearing the evidences that might lead us to her, had gone to great pains to ensure that anyone entering the house did not find anything that could arouse their suspicion. This is not as simple as it appears …,' he said, slipping into a reverie. And just when I thought I had lost him to his thoughts, he turned back sharply to look at me.

'Anyway, I have left Santram to quiz the neighbours and do some snooping around while we check on this girl Rhea,' he said.

I continued eyeing him curiously and, as if getting my drift, he went on to elaborate. 'I had sent someone to the airline office to check if they could provide us with some information about Avantika. The only address they have of her is the Munirka Vihar one. But in the Personal Reference section of the form she had filled at the time of her employment we found a name, a girl called Rhea. There was a mobile number too but Rhea appears to have given up that number and the mobile company had reissued it to someone else. The only lead we now have is Rhea's address. As per the form she was staying in Chhatarpur. Let's hope that she still stays there and is able to shed some light on the matter.'

'Have you heard this name before, Rhea? Did Avantika ever talk about her?' he asked as an afterthought.

'No,' I shook my head gently. Not Rhea, nor any of her other friends, not even her family. Avantika had never had a chance to talk about herself. It was always me or my job or Myra or her condition that we spoke about, never about Avantika. The realisation made me feel as guilty as a driver who had accidently mowed down a bunch of pedestrians under the wheels of his truck.

I learnt from the markings on the shop banners that we had reached Chhatarpur. The area, as Anand explained, was on the outskirts of the city, close to the Delhi – Gurgaon border. Due to its geographic isolation it had been late in getting on to the developmental bandwagon. Land in Chhatarpur had remained inexpensive till the late nineties and some religious trusts, using this to their advantage, had constructed several massive shrines and temples in the area. Educationists, not to be left far behind, had also latched on to the opportunity and erected numerous institutions to cater to the ever-increasing population of Delhi and the resulting demand for education.

It was around these massive structures that residential settlements had sprung up in Chhatarpur, catering to those who derived their livelihood from these establishments or those who could not afford a residence in the heartlands of Delhi. Resultantly, as one strayed from the main roads into the arterial ones, clusters of badly planned dwellings, some with gaudy exteriors and others left barren on the outside, waited in greeting.

Our vehicle, after pausing for directions several times, stopped in front of one such building, an architectural marvel considering that the masons had been able to put together a three storied structure in a plot of land barely enough to park two cars side by side. Right in front of the house was a winding metal staircase that led to the floors above, an obvious encroachment into the narrow street it lined. Understandably the structure could not accommodate an internal stairway.

The dated address of Rhea we were in possession of pegged her to the second floor of the building. We climbed the staircase, Anand in the lead, to reach a landing which had just enough space for two people to stand at a time. I stepped beside Anand as he knocked on the door while the others waited on the metallic steps for the landing to be cleared for their ascension.

The door was bolted from inside. Given the size of the flat, our knocks were probably sounding like hammer strikes to the occupants and yet it was only after five minutes of sustained knocking that we heard a slight shuffle from within. The sound of lazy approaching steps followed and the bolt was disengaged. We waited, as the door stirred with a screech and a face, indolent and sluggish, peered out from the crack.

It was dark inside and that prevented me from making much of the face except that it belonged to a woman. Her questioning gaze shifted from me to Anand and suddenly her eyes widened in alarm. It must have been his uniform, I gathered. She pulled back suddenly and pushed the door, meaning to slam it on our faces. She didn't succeed though, as Anand had already managed to get his foot into the gap. A slight shove and she went stumbling back, leaving the door open for us to enter the dimly lit room.

Eleven

'Who are you? Why have you come here? What do you want?' she screamed. The fear in her voice was evident.

'Shut up!' Anand thundered as he surveyed the walls for the electricity switch. The room was dark, few random rays of sunlight seeping in from the gaps in the drawn curtain serving as the only means of illumination, making it almost impossible to see what lay ahead of us. The air was heavy, laden with smoke, just like the airport smoking lounges.

I coughed and stepped back, fearful at what the woman might resort to. She could have struck us with something. Of whatever I had seen of her she was certainly capable of such flagrancy. Anand had the confidence of his uniform and belief in the fear that his roar would have instilled in her, not me. To me this was like an unexpected teleportation into one of the thriller movies, right in the middle of the climax.

Just then the light came on, a single bulb, wanting in wattage but sufficient to give us an impression of our surroundings. What I saw filled me with instant pity for the habitant, the girl who was staring ludicrously at us, horror writ large in her eyes, mumbling a stream of unintelligible words.

A mattress was spread on the floor, patches of cotton peeping from several gaping holes peppering it, and a pillow, filthy and deformed, rested on it. Barring the few neatly folded garments that rested alongside the most basic toiletry – a soap dish, a toothpaste tube, a brush, a comb and few bottles of nail paint and eye liners – atop the wooden table in the corner, all other clothes she owned were strewn across the floor.

Dirty utensils were piled up against one wall, some of them harbouring liberal fungal growth on the scraps that hadn't been washed off them. An empty can of milk powder had been converted into an ashtray and rested on the floor, overflowing with ash, cigarette butts and half-burnt matchsticks. I was certain that there were several items in the room which were emitting stenches of their own and had it not been for the overpowering smell of cigarette smoke, we would have been forced to flee holding our noses.

'It is that *Harami* Satish who has sent you here, no? Please don't listen to... to... that slimy son of a bitch. I haven't done anything *Saheb*. He takes away all my money... How am I to eat then, tell me? If I don't go to a customer or two without informing him, how will I ever manage to make ends meet? Everything has become so expensive these days. Even a bloody packet of mint costs twenty rupees,' she persisted with her incessant blabbering. One moment she would sound like a rebel and the very next she would be pleading with Anand.

'Shut up or I will drag you to the station and lock you up for good,' Anand screamed once again. The effect was magical. Instantly she sealed her lips and continued eyeing him as a hapless sheep would eye the butcher. It was then that I saw her long enough to take notice.

She had a face which had been ignored into ageing. Beneath her dreamy eyes were puddles as dark as her long lashes, and several other blemishes on her skin spoke of the abuse she must have endured. The translucent negligee she wore did little to conceal a body that would once have set tongues wagging. She wasn't grossly out of shape even now, but the burn marks around her thighs, several small circles, like she had at some point taken to using her own body for extinguishing cigarettes, took away most of her appeal. In my best estimate she would be in her mid to late twenties, at least half a decade younger than the impression one was likely to get with only a casual glance.

'We haven't been sent here by Satish or by anyone else for that matter. We need some information from you and that is why we are here. If you cooperate with us and tell us what we want to know, we will go back just as we came, without harming you in any way. But if you believe you are too smart and wish to test that hypothesis now, I promise you that your sorry ass will be relinquished to the darkest cells of Tihar Jail and you will remain there till your last living breath,' Anand said. His tone was consolatory, but the underlying menace in the words was apparent. I felt goose bumps emerging at the back of my neck.

The girl nodded meekly.

'Is your name Rhea Bhattacharya?'

She nodded again.

'How long have you been living here?'

'For the past eight years.'

Anand was a seasoned interrogator and I got a glimpse of his finesse in the manner that he went about quizzing Rhea. He asked her several objective questions, the kind where she would not have a reason to lie, and when she had let her guard down, he asked her if she knew Avantika.

'Avantika who… Avantika Rathore?' she returned. 'Yes I knew her, but that was a long time back,' she said after Anand's confirmatory nod.

Anand continued showering her with questions and Rhea answered unabashedly. One of them did not know Avantika at all while the other, in her own admittance, had known her a long way back in time. This made the discussion extremely impersonal, like they were talking about a world event or any other occurrence that they both held an opinion on.

But for me Avantika was an object of flesh and blood, she was someone I had fallen for and not yet managed to share my feelings with. As a result what I heard from Rhea left me numbed. As she went on with her narrative, I felt her words boring through me like a drilling machine. Somewhere along the line I lost sense of place and time and sat down on the same mucky mattress that I had once thought to be unfit for human use. Both Anand and Rhea gave me a fleeting glance, distracted by my sudden need to rest my trembling legs, before resuming their dialogue.

Avantika and Rhea, I learnt, were flat mates during college, about nine years in the past. It was one of those private hostels in South Extension that stuffs girl students and working women by the dozen to a flat. The two girls in question shared the same room and were enrolled in separate colleges of Delhi University's South Campus. Rhea was from West Bengal while Avantika had come from somewhere in Rajasthan.

Despite Anand's insistence, Rhea could not divulge even the name of the city, let alone provide an address, which could point towards Avantika's antecedents.

Like is often the case, within their first few months in Delhi they were both smitten by the big-city razzle-dazzle, glitz and glamour. One following the other, their sense of dressing, their mannerisms and their small-town mindset began to metamorphose, preparing them for dissolving into the waters of feigned freedom which is both used and misused by young migrants ever so often.

They were both young, pretty and had the able guidance of other girls from the hostel who had already adapted themselves to this 'modern' lifestyle. So, it was only a matter of time that they became regulars at some of the most exclusive pubs and discotheques in town, with eligible men, rich and handsome, biting out of their hands wherever they went. Being driven around the streets of Delhi in fast swanky cars and dining at expensive restaurants, on their date's tab of course, became an everyday affair. And before they realised, the two simple girls who had come to Delhi in pursuit of education had been reduced to a hazy memory from the distant past.

Rhea admitted that it was she who had been the first to succumb to her temptations.

Some girls from the hostel, in a bid to provide for their ever demanding lifestyles, had come up with an arrangement to substantiate their meagre pocket money or salaries, as was the case. On certain evenings these girls would vanish abruptly, not to be seen in the hostel before break of the next dawn. And when they returned, they would be brandishing expensive phones, jewellery or other items of value which they otherwise could not have dreamt of affording.

'It was odd, but we were both new to the setting and hence were not in a position to question them. We had our suspicions about their engagements and sometimes Avantika and I would discuss them in private,' Rhea explained.

It was later, when the two had taken their first steps towards leading life in the fast lane, that the arrangement was disclosed to them confirming their worst suspicions. The girls were indeed engaged in the oldest form of occupation known to mankind, prostitution. They however preferred calling their profession Escort Services, reacting rather indignantly to any of the other patronising term used to describe it.

When you remain in the proximity of evil for long, it tends to lose its maliciousness in your eyes. Such was the case with the two impressionable girls. The lure of riches and glamour eventually got to them, blinding them to the perils of their industry and permitting the sin to seep in through the barricades of their morality.

Rhea was the first one to step into the muck. Her youthful effervescence and novelty made her an instant hit with the clients. In a short span of time she found herself travelling to several cities – Ahmedabad, Bhopal, Patna, Chennai and Hyderabad – on day trips, leaving early in the morning and returning by the evening, leaving behind a bunch of spent and content customers wherever she went. She soon got herself a full-time manager, a sophisticated pimp, who helped her rake in the green.

'Avantika wasn't made for this profession. She was the typical girl who likes to lose herself in a world of her fantasies. She was a romantic at heart. She warned me several times too, that I was spoiling my life, my future... I wish I had listened to her... But I was too greedy for that. I had tasted blood and there was no turning back. So, instead I reasoned with her, persistently, until she was dragged into this muck too,' Rhea said. There was sadness in her eyes, the sadness stemming from her inability to alter decisions she had made in the past. She could only live to rue them now.

'But how did that happen? If she wasn't made for the profession, how did you ever manage to talk her into it?' I heard myself speak. There was a look of surprise on Anand's face at my sudden interjection but the words had been a sort of an instantaneous reaction. My angst and scepticism had made me seek an explanation.

'She was seeing someone at that time, a guy we had met at one of the nightclubs. He was into garment exports, if I recall correctly. He had approached offering to buy us a round of drinks and we had allowed him to join us. He sounded suave and cultured, unlike the brash and arrogant fellows who keep hopping from bar to bar in search of a catch. I could see a sparkle of interest in Avantika's eyes in the very first meeting and I wasn't wrong. Soon they were a pair, inseparable and devoted.

Their relationship lasted for about eight months and then something went wrong. I think it was right after Avantika's return from a visit to her hometown that they broke off. It took a terrible toll on her, as if someone had brutally snatched away her zest for life. I tried to get her to talk, but she didn't. She could be extremely obstinate when it came to certain things. If she didn't wish to talk about something, you couldn't get it out of her using a suction pump…'

'What was this guy's name? Which part of Delhi was he from?' Anand sliced in.

She shook her head sideways. 'Too much time and too many men have passed by ever since for me to be able to recall.'

Once Anand acknowledged her response with a nod, she turned in the general direction of my seated form and continued, 'It was around that time that I got this assignment in Mumbai. One of my regular customers wanted to entertain his European buyers and had approached my manager to arrange for two girls. The manager in turn had left it upon me to decide who I wanted to take along. I was about to ask one of our other flat-mates but something made me bring it up with Avantika. I was certain she would decline, but to my utter dismay, she agreed. She came with me to Mumbai and that was the first time she got paid for extending sexual favours.

She didn't speak to me on our return flight, not a single casual word, and I thought that the shock had proven too much for her to handle. I was positive that her career as an Escort had ended with the very first assignment and once again she managed to surprise me. About a week later, she asked me to have a word with my manager and arrange an assignment for her. Obviously, I couldn't turn her down.

She took to it, but strictly on her own terms. She would take on only two to three assignments in a month, a pittance when compared with the twenty-odd I was managing, and would quiz the manager extensively before agreeing to entertain any new customer. So often the manager, Satish, would come to me cribbing about a client that Avantika had turned down or a high-paying assignment she had backed out from. And that is why I said that she wasn't cut out for this job…'

Rhea went on speaking and I continued listening, trying not to explode under the burden of the shocking discovery. Surprisingly, the fact that Avantika had only been a part-time whore didn't make me feel any better.

Rhea, I learnt, had not only made a name for herself in her chosen profession but had also amassed plenty of wealth in little time. Her humble upbringing had taught her to secure her ends while she was still capable of doing so and so she bought a small flat, the one where Anand was engaged in interrogating her now, and moved out of the hostel.

For the first few years things went just as she had hoped they would, but slowly her sheen began to wear off. The very customers who would once spare no efforts in proclaiming their love for her had now resorted to beating her down on the charges, looking for a bargain, and by now she was entrenched too deep into it to resist. She had begun smoking sometime back and now she found herself drinking heavily. It was a medium for her to escape from the reality, a source of comfort in her rapidly diminishing career.

As her mind got habituated to the alcohol's buzz, it began craving for even harder forms of inebriants and she obliged. Weed, Hashish and eventually Cocaine, she switched from one potent remedy to the other, but her pain refused to let go. The only purpose they did serve though was to act as a catalyst and accelerate her downfall. Soon there were hardly any customers left, no surprise given how different the girl staring at her from the mirror was to her own earlier self.

Even Satish, the man who had once earned his bread off Rhea, did not remain unaffected. He started avoiding her, often refusing to take her calls, and her desperate pleas for money or a customer who was desperate enough to pay for sleeping with her were forced to remain muffled within her. When he did take her call or on the rare occasions that he paid her a visit, he would be excessively abusive and aggressive.

To substantiate her words, Rhea turned around to show us the bruises she carried on her back from Satish's last visit. It was a pathetic sight. Repulsive and pitiful! As if earning a living out of peddling girls was not enough, this guy was even scaling inhuman heights with his brutality.

'After I left the hostel we kept in touch, sporadically though, for about a year or so. But eventually we got immersed in our respective lives and drifted apart. Last I know, she had started working for an airline company,' she surmised.

Anand, after some more questions and a by-the-way warning for her to keep away from trouble, indicated that the purpose of our visit had been served and we could start out. As he made for the door, followed closely by his aides, I fell back a step. Pulling out a five hundred rupee note, I slipped it into her hands unobtrusively. There was a flicker of hesitation, but she was quick to overcome it and seize the currency, giving me a mixed look of astonishment and gratitude.

'Is Avantika in some kind of trouble?' she whispered. Having found one sympathetic soul among the invaders, she had mustered the courage to voice her curiosity and maybe concern even. Ignoring the question, I stepped out of the door and followed the lady constable down the stairway.

'If you keep doling out notes to her kind, it is only a matter of time before you will land up outside the Jama Masjid, begging,' Anand nudged once we were comfortably seated in the backseat of his vehicle.

I thought I had been discreet, but obviously I hadn't succeeded in cheating his trained eyes. I smiled back in response.

It was hard for me to explain the sudden surge of sympathy for Rhea to my own self, let alone Anand. I had felt stifled all the while I was in her apartment, by the surroundings, by her and by the story she had to tell. Plus, it wasn't like the old days any more. The money meant a substantial bit to me now, an equivalent of the pre-paid cab fare from the Mumbai airport to my residence. As a consequence of my action, I had committed myself to standing in the auto queue instead, but I harboured no remorse. I knew that Rhea would find better use for the money.

'She might be buying herself a nice strong fix with your money right now,' he quipped, as if he had heard my thoughts somehow. I chose to remain silent.

'It's been difficult for you, I understand, but what fun would life be if it were to be devoid of its complexities? In my line of work, on an everyday basis, I come across people who are faced with worse. And all of them have to move on eventually, either willingly or unwillingly. Gather yourself and move on, you have much to live for, Myra for instance…,' he said after a while. His tone was sombre and consolatory now. I nodded.

'So, what is it that you intend to do now? I am certain we will manage to trace her, but the pursuit might take some time. Do you intend to stay put in Delhi till then or would you be returning to Mumbai?' he continued.

He was right. There was no point staying back. I had no idea how many days it would take before Avantika was found. Moreover, I couldn't let Myra stay with Rashmi for much longer. I needed to be by her side and figure out a way to raise the money. Anand was going to persist with the hunt, he had assured me, and I could always come back if I was required to.

'I think I will return to Mumbai and wait to hear from you… It doesn't make sense for me to stay back… Can you drop me someplace from where I can hail an auto to the airport?' I replied.

'Yes, but what time is your flight?'

'I haven't got my return bookings done as yet. I think I will go the airport and get a ticket over the counter itself.'

Anand dropped me somewhere near the IIT Gate, and the very first auto driver I spoke with agreed to ferry me to my destination. It was a surprise, considering the notoriety of the species I had experienced firsthand over the past couple of days. Perhaps the fact that I had got down from a Delhi Police vehicle or that I had been given a warm hug by an officer in uniform just before approaching him might have helped him make up his mind.

The auto began its sprint, veering and swerving past the sea of vehicles that made up the chaotic Delhi traffic and I felt as if the world around, including the rickety sound of the auto, was gradually blotting out. Once again I was lost in Avantika's thoughts. Only the warmth that I was used to experiencing whenever I thought about her had been displaced by a feeling of frustrated fury.

Why had she done this? She had no right to mingle into our lives and keep such a crucial fact hidden from us. What was I to tell Myra, that her Avantika Aunty was a retired prostitute?

It wasn't a one-dimensional deliberation. There was a feeble voice within my head which was offering counter-arguments as well, desperately trying to shield Avantika. What she did was her past, one that she has moved away from. What purpose, other than prodding her old wounds, would be served by bringing it up now? Would you have given her the place in your life that you did had you been aware of her past? Would you have permitted her to get as close to Myra as she was now?

There were no answers, only questions, like a clew of worms, tangling and jumbling within my head. One moment I would be disgusted with Avantika, images of strange hands, belonging to grungy old men, feeling the body that had hitherto held a sanctified appeal for me, flashing before my eyes. The very next instant I would find myself trying to empathise with her situation and defending her standpoint. It was a tug of war and even as

I involuntarily embarked upon it, I knew that there could not emerge a victor.

'No matter what her past, would you deny that she stood by your side in your hour of need? Would you deny that she filled the void for Myra that her own mother had created by abandoning her?' I suddenly heard the voice within my head say. It was no longer sounding as frail as it had done initially. Perhaps the conviction behind its arguments was lending it strength. 'Just for that, don't you think it is your responsibility to do whatever you can to trace her? For all you know she might be in some sort of a jam and in need of your help... Really? Have you actually done all that you could to find her? Think again!' it continued.

And then it struck me. There was one thing I hadn't done, something that no one but I could do. I hadn't been able to ascertain whether Shalini or her family had anything to do with Avantika's disappearance.

'Wait! Take me to Sainik Farms first,' I heard myself instructing the auto driver.

'We have nearly reached the airport *Saheb*... Sainik Farms is in the opposite direction. We will have to travel all the way back...,' he lodged a meek protest but I wasn't in the mood to negotiate.

Grudgingly, he took a U-turn and began racing back the very roads he had just covered. In about an hour I was in Sainik Farms, right outside the bungalow that had once belonged to my in-laws, intent on doing my last bit for Avantika. The auto driver, smelling a fortune of a fare, had agreed to wait and take me back to the airport when I got done. He was parked on the other end of the road and had already lit up a bidi by the time I ambled across to the gate.

'Good afternoon *Saheb*,' the guard greeted me with his customary nasal twang. I noticed the flash of recognition on his face turn to apprehension. He knew who I was (or had been) and he was probably aware of all that had transpired since I used to be a welcome guest to the bungalow. He was therefore uncertain of how he should react to my presence. He too, like the servant inside, was a man governed by orders and no one had told him what he needed to do if I were to suddenly show up at the gate.

Using his confusion to my benefit, I muttered something to the effect that I was expected inside and steered past him, through the grass lawn, towards the red brick structure. If I had allowed the guard to seek instructions from his controllers, I was certain that he would have been fed some or the other excuse to prevent me from entering. He would make the call nevertheless but now that I was inside the premises already, I could hope that courtesy would prevail and I would not be forcefully evacuated.

I pushed open the large wooden door that opened into the living area, an extravagantly plush set-up as I remembered it from my earlier visits. The adornments had not changed much, and perched on the large leather lounger, remotely switching channels on the wall-mounted television, was the familiar frame of Shalini.

'You?' she exclaimed, as I barged into the scene.

From the corner of my eye I caught the house-help, who had been occupied in dusting the brass artefacts scattered across the hall earlier, sneaking up the staircase.

'What are you doing here?' Shalini followed up.

'I need to speak to you and since you wouldn't take my calls, I thought it was best that I visit you in person,' I replied nonchalantly, somewhat relishing the discomfort that my presence caused her.

'But I don't want to speak to you,' she shot back furiously.

'Guess what, neither do I. But sadly there are certain things that warrant a discussion. A discussion cannot be avoided, irrespective of how we feel about engaging in one.'

'In that case why don't you have that discussion with me?' I heard a booming voice behind me. My ex-father-in-law was climbing down the last few steps of the staircase to arrive into the hall. His faithful servant was trailing close behind. 'Shalu, go back in,' he commanded and Shalini rushed to follow his orders.

It wasn't only his thundering voice, but his entire personality – tall and lanky with a face as hard as rock and perfectly matching expressions – was capable of instilling fear in anybody who dared confront him. On another day I would have meekly bowed a retreat, but not today. Today I was fuelled by a purpose too weighty to be cowed down by any human presence, no matter how foreboding.

'I am here to talk about Avantika. I am not sure if you know her,' I replied, looking him straight in the eye.

'Incidentally I do recall having heard that name. So, go on, tell me what is it about her that you wish to talk?'

'During my last conversation with Shalini, she had admonished Avantika vociferously, threatening of dire consequences if she remained in contact with Myra. Since then Avantika has gone missing… While the police are doing their bit to locate her, I came here to check if Shalini actually had something to do with it.' I had deliberately mentioned the police for effect, in the hope that it would help earn his cooperation. It did not.

'If the police are already looking for her, let them do their job. I am sure they are efficient enough to be able to track the girl. Why come here then?' he retorted.

His voice was calm as a cucumber and yet shrilling enough to give me goose bumps. He had not refuted my allegation and nor had he reacted heatedly as any normal person, wrongly accused of a crime would. I had explicitly said that I had come to check if Shalini had anything to do with Avantika's disappearance and he had chosen to ignore the statement completely. Maybe Shalini did have something to do with it after all. Maybe it was him who had orchestrated the felony on behalf of his daughter.

'Avantika has nothing to do with this. The fight is between Shalini and me, so please keep Avantika out of this. If you have any information about where she is, share it with me now and we can both forget that this discussion ever happened,' I pushed on.

'You forget Rahul; this is not just about you and Shalini. There is another soul involved, Myra, my granddaughter,' he replied with an impish smile.

There was something about the smile that made a shiver run up my spine. With every sentence he spoke, my conviction that it was he who was responsible for Avantika vanishing only strengthened. Seeing him smile, a sudden thought occurred to me – Avantika was missing for well over a fortnight now. Who would kidnap a girl and keep her for that long without making even an attempt to use her as leverage for achieving some other objective? What if he had already eliminated Avantika?

I didn't have to wait long for an answer. When he spoke again, his voice had acquired a negotiating but severe tone.

'Myra's illness requires money, a lot of it, which you don't have. Let us face it; you are not even in a position to provide for her in the manner that she is accustomed to leading her life. So, why do you want to sacrifice your own daughter's future for the sake of your ego? Why don't you give her to Shalini and let her have the life she deserves?' he said.

I felt an instant urge to scream at him, but checking myself with much effort, I said, 'This is not about Myra. We have debated all these points in court before I was awarded her custody. In case you are not satisfied with the decision and wish to challenge it, you are free to do so. Right now the only thing I am interested in discussing is Avantika's release.'

'Don't be so naïve Rahul. All issues, irrespective of whether or not you are interested in discussing them, are linked to Myra's custody only. Hand over her custody to Shalini and everything,

I repeat, everything, will turn out exactly the way you have been hoping.'

'Are you saying that you will release Avantika only if I hand over Myra's custody? Is this some kind of blackmail?' My temper was already pressing hard against my composure, looking for the slightest fissure to flare up.

'Now, those are your words, not mine. I never said that this girl, Avantika, or whatever she is called, is in my captivity. But yes, I can assure you that I will try my level best to ensure her safe release. And you must know by now that whenever I try to do something wholeheartedly, it usually happens.' He still had that vicious smile of his affixed to his face.

My head was throbbing, as though all the blood in my veins had decided to congregate there.

Of course this was blackmail. My shrewd ex-father-in-law had said all that he wanted to without even admitting to the crime. No wonder he was making such a resounding success of his political career. He had in abundance all the essential ingredients required for it.

He had craftily passed the buck over to me. The decision was now mine and it dwarfed even the most complex problems of algebra and trigonometry.

'There is no hurry. Go back home and think this through. I will give you three days to make up your mind. In a week's time I will have my lawyers draw up the papers and you can bring Myra along when you come to sign them. Of course Myra will remain here, receiving the best medical attention and other material comforts that money can buy, while you can return to your old life.

I will also have a word with your erstwhile employers and see if they could take you back once again. And in case, by some inexplicable surge of hormones you decide against taking up this offer, well, God be with you and with those whom you care for.'

He had just issued a threat. The one meaning I was able to gather from his words was that if I did not hand over Myra's custody to Shalini, he would have Avantika killed. The only respite he had allowed me was that I wasn't required to make a decision immediately. I had three days to do so.

Quietly, I turned on my heels and made for the door. I was left with little doubt about Avantika's whereabouts and though I had several things going on in my head, I didn't want to utter them and make the situation worse for either Avantika or for my own self. I was no longer in control of the discussion. Somewhere along the way he had snatched the reins of the conversation from me. I needed to get out as soon as I could and get a grip on my thoughts.

'Rahul,' I heard him call out while I was still a few steps away from the door. I stopped and turned just a little so I didn't have to face him.

'Just a word of advice from someone who has seen a lot more of life than you: base your decision on nothing but what is good for your daughter. Your job, Avantika, all these are incidental, what is most crucial is that Myra gets the treatment and the upbringing she deserves. If you base your decision on any other factor, a situation might arise where you are left to struggle with the burden of your decision for the rest of your life. And the pain of such regret, my son, is the worst that any human being can inflict upon his or her own self.'

Twelve

Myra was elated to see me when I reached Rashmi's house to receive her. Her first words however were, 'Did you find Avantika Aunty?'

During the flight back from Delhi, I had managed to stall Avantika's thoughts from invading my brain. I had used the recent discovery about her past to convince myself that she didn't quite deserve the importance and attention I was bestowing upon her. Plus, I had more urgent matters to tend to. Shalini's father's words were ceaselessly ringing in my ears and as much as I felt like rubbishing them, I couldn't entirely refute their factuality.

I could continue living in my delirium and believe that everything would get back to normal, but the fact was that I had lost the most significant battle of my life. I was a nobody now, a man without a career and without any money. What could be worse, I wasn't even in a state to provide for my own daughter. Shalini had left me and Avantika had too. Perhaps both of them had good reasons for doing so. After all who would have the patience to indefinitely tolerate a loser?

No, I wasn't giving up hope. Had I not held on to it at the very worst of times - when Shalini left me or when I lost my job or even when the doctor told me about Myra's illness? I had. Why then would I suddenly slip into a piteous state of despair now? I wasn't losing hope; I was only coming to terms with reality.

The truth was that my daughter needed a bone marrow transplant, a procedure that would cost a quantum of money I didn't have and hadn't been able to raise. No matter how much I screamed that I would do anything for my daughter and that I would find the money 'somehow', reality was that I had no idea how or where to find it. So then, was I, in some absurdly conceited manner, risking Myra's life by wanting to cling on to her? Had her custody become more important to me than her well-being? Was I being too selfish, unwilling to let go of my own happiness for the sake of my daughter's?

The answer was simple. The only way out for me was to return Myra to Shalini and settle for an arrangement where I could visit her whenever I wanted to. Maybe I could also bargain for a clause entitling me to bring her back to Mumbai during her vacations.

The trouble was that the sustained separation had somewhat alienated Myra from Shalini. She no longer missed her mother as she had done earlier. She never enquired about her return, having accepted and adjusted with her fate. I couldn't deny that the hatred Shalini had induced in me with her actions might have subconsciously rubbed on to my daughter as well, making it all the more difficult for her to agree to stay with Shalini now.

Myra wasn't going to agree to relocate to Delhi and forcing her to do so, against her wishes, was not the right thing to do, especially in light of her health concerns. I had to figure a way to alter her feelings about her mother and her maternal grandparents, to get her to warm up to them once again, and I had just about a week to accomplish all of this.

I decided to begin straight away, with the first words I said to her in response to her question.

'No, we haven't been able to locate Avantika Aunty as yet, but she will be found soon. Both your Momma and your Nanu are looking for her in Delhi and they will surely be able to find her,' I said.

She thought for a while, as if digesting my reply, before enquiring in a near whisper. 'You met Momma in Delhi?'

'Yes, I met her and she was asking about you. I told her how well you have been performing at school and she was elated,' I said, forcing a look of excitement.

'Then why did she never come to see me?' Her voice was still measured and low-pitched.

'She said she will come to see you… soon… And if she doesn't come, we will both go to Delhi and see her,' I replied. Myra did not respond and in her eyes I could see a hint of confusion. I hadn't succeeded in convincing her. Not to the slightest bit. I could see the challenge ahead of me and it made me cringe. The next week promised to be a trying one and I wasn't particularly looking forward to it.

That night I barely managed to sleep. I kept staring at Myra's peaceful form lying alongside me on the bed, admiring her face, her features, some of which she had inherited from me. She was a lovely little thing, one meant to be pampered and loved. She had lost quite a bit of weight over the past few months but that could all be reversed once her treatment was taken care of.

I reminisced the day Myra was born, a small tightly wrapped bundle that the nurse had thrust into my arms, I remembered the first intelligible word she had spoken, Papa, and I recalled, with a smile, the day she had managed her first set of unaided steps. In that one night, I wanted to relive every joyous moment that Myra had brought into my life, suppressing the nibbling thorn embedded deep within my heart.

In that one night, I had become one with all those parents, poor folks from remote villages, who are forced to sell their children for the sake of their own sustenance. Till then I had only come across such stories while flipping through newspapers and had invariably regarded them with utter indifference and triviality. That is, if I had ever regarded them at all. But today I had become one of them. I was taking the very step they were compelled to take and was feeling exactly as they would have felt. Their suffocating frustration and helplessness was no longer alien to me, it had now become a composite part of my wretched existence.

It was around eleven the next morning when the call came.

To Myra's delight, I had suggested that she skip school for the next few days, an offer she had jumped on to. I even called up Arden and, briefly explaining the situation at hand, informed him of my absence from work for the week to follow. He didn't voice his concerns, but I could hear them in his unspoken words. I was stretching things too far with him. I had been taking his graciousness for granted, I knew, but I wish I had another option.

We had just finished gorging on the mooli parathas prepared by the maid, a late, lazy breakfast, and were engaged in some casual banter, mostly Myra filling me on the things she had been up to while I was in Delhi, when my mobile phone rang. It was a Mumbai number, an unknown landline connection. I was in half mood to disconnect the call, but on an instinct I ended up taking it.

'Am I speaking to Mr. Rahul Singh?' a well-groomed female voice enquired.

'Yes,' I said, half hoping that it was one of those tele-callers trying to sell me a loan.

'I am calling from Mr. Ramesh Sethmalani's office…,' she offered, putting to rest my assumptions about her identity. 'The lawyer…,' she added as an afterthought.

Of course! Who hadn't heard of Ramesh Sethmalani? He was one of the most prominent legal eagles of the country. When he was not arguing high-profile cases in the courtroom, he could be found verbally assaulting his fellow panelists on one or the other television channel discussions. The question was that what did Ramesh Sethmalani want from me?

'Yes?' I said, slightly circumspect suddenly.

'Mr. Sethmalani would like to see you on an urgent matter. Would it be possible for you to make it to our office sometime later today?'

It took me a few seconds to recover from the shock. There was no fathomable reason for a lawyer of his repute to wish to see me, unless of course his firm had been hired by someone to do so. The list of people who might need the mediation of a legal expert to speak to me wasn't particularly long. And when I narrowed it down to those who could afford Mr. Sethmalani's fees, I was left with only one name. Shalini's!

It wasn't adding up though. Why would she have a lawyer speak to me when two days were still left of the deadline her father had given me?

Maybe it was just a distasteful prank. There were several radio shows garnering listenership by way of such pranks. It could well be a twisted idea of amusement that some people I knew were capable of conjuring. Poka for instance! Had Poka returned to Mumbai by any chance? Could he lend me the money I needed?

'Madam, you seriously don't think that you will call me claiming that you are representing a prominent lawyer I have no dealings with and I will come running to wherever you want me to, do you?' I heard myself say.

'I do understand your apprehensions Mr. Singh, but one of our clients has left something for you with us. And we have specific instructions to hand it over to you in person, in our own office. Else, we would have gladly sent it to your address… However, to ascertain my identity, you could take down our phone number and call us back. You will need to ask for Karishma,' she said.

Her words left me in little doubt that she was indeed telling the truth. I could have taken her number and called her back, but that would have been an exercise in futility. Instead, I tried to quiz Karishma about the package and the nameless client of theirs who wanted it delivered to me, but to no avail. She did not divulge an iota more of information than she had already shared, except for the directions to her office.

In two hours of receiving the call, I was sitting in the waiting area of Ramesh Sethmalani's office in the Fort area of Mumbai. The office was housed in one of the many remaining buildings from the British era. Its exteriors, though still sturdy, spoke of many years of continued neglect. The paint was peeling off in several places and conspicuous dark patches of erosion peppered its façade. I had to climb only two floors through the badly lit staircase but the unevenly set stone steps had left me panting for breath.

The scenery drastically changed once I pushed open the heavy wooden doors proclaiming, in carved brass alphabets, to house the offices of 'Sethmalani and Sons'. It was as plush and contemporary as any office I had ever been to. Yellow lights peeping from the false ceiling, leather sofas, and an MF Husain painting adorning one of the walls made it seem like a hotel lobby rather than the law firm office it was.

The wait wasn't long. Within few minutes of the receptionist relegating me to one of the sofas, a door opened and a girl in a black business suit walked in. Glancing at the receptionist and catching her nod, she came to where I was sitting and introduced herself as Karishma. Yes, the voice was the same. She would be an intern, I guessed by her youthful appearance.

'Mr. Sethmalani is waiting for you,' she said and guided me along a passageway lined with unmarked doors. Eight of them, I counted. She stopped in front of the last door to our right and in one swift motion knocked and pushed it open. Inside, behind a large desk, was the face I had seen many-a-times on the television.

'Mr. Rahul Singh, Sir,' the girl announced and left the room.

The lawyer, a jolly-faced, heavily built man with a receding hairline - just the kind of look that would make his adversaries let their guard down in the courtroom - got up from his seat with great effort and after shaking my hands, slumped back down.

'Please Mr. Singh, have a seat,' he said, still eyeing the bunch of papers lying on his desk. He sifted through them and then, abruptly putting them aside, looked straight into my eyes.

'I assume you know Miss Avantika Rathore,' he said.

I would have looked like a moron staring back at him with an open mouth but Avantika's was the last name I was expecting to hear. Taking a few moments to gather my wits, I nodded in the affirmative. 'Do you know her too? Is she the same client of yours that Karishma was referring to? Do you know where she is?' a series of questions came tumbling out as soon as I regained my voice.

'Yes, Mr. Singh. The answer to all your questions is yes. But instead of getting me to address your curiosity, why don't you take a look at this,' he said, extending an envelope towards me. I didn't know from where the envelope had materialised. I hadn't seen it lying on the desk and neither had he taken it out of a drawer.

'This should tell you all that you wish to know,' he added once I had taken custody of the envelope.

Hurriedly, I tore it open and pulled out a bunch of neatly stapled sheets, about four or five of them. Instead of looking at the text printed on them, curious, I shifted my gaze towards the lawyer once again.

'Read it,' he goaded, signalling with a slight sway of his head towards the papers I was holding.

Following his instructions, I unfolded the document and began reading it. It was easily the most perturbing and also the most treasured piece of text I have ever read. It was a letter from Avantika.

'Dear Rahul,' it began. I stared at my name for a fraction longer than was needed before moving on.

'You might have wondered as to where I am or why did I suddenly have to disappear. Myra must have been worried too. I know I owe you both an apology, but more than that I owe you an explanation. An explanation that may or may not be to your satisfaction, but one that my conscience won't allow me to evade. Several times I have tried to tell you about myself, my past, which has cast a shadow so dark that all I can see ahead of me is obscurity and more darkness.

As is so often the case, when one tries too hard to talk about something, repeating and rehearsing the lines in our mind till the illusion of perfection sets in, we are betrayed by the very words that we believe to have tamed. I was too. I never could muster the courage to disturb the nameless relationship we had unknowingly embarked upon. It was a mistake, keeping you in the dark, I knew, but little Myra and you had become too precious for me to take a chance with. And today, when I am committed to correcting my error, I want to start at the very beginning and not hold back on anything. Please be patient with me Rahul…'

I looked up. The rage I had been gradually nursing within me had miraculously melted away already. I felt a strong urge to look her in the eye and say that I was already aware of the past she was alluding to. I had met Rhea and through her I had discovered the muck from her past that Avantika had struggled to bring up. It was her past, and who doesn't have a skeleton or two hidden in their closet? I wanted to tell her that it didn't mean a thing, certainly not something so drastic that obligated her to abandon us. But she wasn't there.

Instead I saw Sethmalani's intense gaze scrutinising me. It was as if he were studying every little reaction of mine, every frown and every crease that appeared on my face as a consequence of the letter. Somewhat unsettled, I turned my attention back to the letter.

'I was born in Surajpur Estate near Jodhpur in Rajasthan. My father, Ranvir Singh, was the eldest son of Late Rai Bahadur Tej

Singh Rathore, a name you might come across in some chronicles of the struggle for India's independence. I never saw my mother. She died while giving birth to me, a natural barter that didn't go very well with my father.

My father never married again despite continued pressure from his family, which lasted even while I had started attending school. He pampered me like any doting father would, teaching me to ride a horse and taking me with him for his visits to the fields. But in my mother he had lost not only the woman he loved but also his hopes for a son, a legal heir who would take his bloodline forward, and the resulting gloom never left his eyes. He didn't blame me for my mother's death, but soon enough I had matured sufficiently to make my own deductions.

The guilt made me overly sensitive to slightest of things – a whisper being exchanged between my grandmother and my aunt or even a perfectly reasonable scolding from my father – everything appeared to me as an insinuation of my mother's death, a crime that I was responsible for. My guilt was stifling me within my own home and so, the first opportunity for an escape that came my way, I grabbed at it with both hands.

I moved to Delhi to pursue my graduation. My father wasn't pleased with the idea, girls in our family weren't known to pursue academics, let alone step out of the house before marriage, but a mother not being in the equation, I had mastered the art of bargaining with him by then.

Delhi was a life changing experience in more ways than one. I had moved into a paying guest accommodation in South Extension which provided food and shelter, at an obnoxious price of course, to outstation girls who were either studying or struggling to make a career in Delhi. These objectives however were merely a front, a rationale they gave to their families for staying in the city, whereas in reality they had but a singular objective: To live life at their own terms.

Most of them, in coming to Delhi, had broken away from years of restrain that their hometowns had imposed upon them. They also knew that in a few years, the shackles of marriage would once again bind them to the life of drudgery they had escaped from. The escape was only momentary and the zeal to make the most of it meant heavy socialising, partying like there was no tomorrow, drinking, going out with boys and a host of other things. I was young, impressionable and coming from a similar background as most of them. It was therefore only natural that I became one with them before I could even realise.

It was then that I met Sandeep. He was a rare combination of good looks, noble upbringing and money he could claim to have earned himself (he had started working in his family business at an early age). I was smitten, full credit to him since he left no stone unturned to ensure that I was. We would go out to the fanciest of places, hold hands while watching a movie, look into each other's eyes through a flickering candle at the dinner table and a host of other things that young couples usually engage in. I will spare you the nitty-gritties, as I am sure you are no stranger to them yourself'.

I couldn't help but smile. She was obviously alluding to the days when I was courting Shalini. I had shared with Avantika several episodes from my life back then, not bothering even once to enquire about her life in turn. The smile vanished as soon as it had surfaced and I was back to reading again.

'I would thank God every day for his special consideration. While the girls around me had to surround themselves with boys to extract the joy they desired from life, in my case it had come about effortlessly. Sandeep was both my means and my end and there were times I would have to pinch myself to believe that it was all for real and not just a dream. We would talk about our life together, marriage, travelling to the remotest corners of the world and growing old in each other's company. We had even shortlisted the names for our babies, a boy and a girl.

It was all so nice that I feared losing it. In my own guileless manner I wanted to get a stamp of approval for our relationship, something that would further strengthen the bonds that held us together, and therefore, without letting Sandeep know of my intentions, I headed back home to talk to my father. I knew he would object, but I was confident that I would manage to convince him eventually. That is the way things had worked all through my life.

Only when I spoke to him did I realise that this was not something as trivial as getting him to buy me a new dress, or permission to spend the night at a friend's place, or even convincing him to permit me to go to Delhi. This was the most significant decision that he, in his capacity as my father, was going to make for me. Considerations like caste, culture and background, factors that I hadn't even bothered myself with, suddenly became paramount and my father refused to budge from his stance. He even threatened to cut short my stay in Delhi and get me back to Surajpur if I didn't listen to him. "You will marry a Rajput boy who is aware of our customs and culture, not some Baniya from Delhi. And that is final," he had said before storming out of the room.

We hardly ever spoke after that discussion and I, in the hope that he might have a change of heart, went on extending my stay at home. Sandeep would call once in a while but, in the fear that my father would find out, I found myself barely able to hold the conversation for a minute or two. The situation was in a state of limbo and something had to give soon. And that it did.

I was closing in on a week of unfruitful stay at home when I realised that my periods should have come a few days back. They were nowhere in sight. The cramps and contractions in my stomach, my ever so loyal harbingers of four days of impending gloom, were nowhere in sight either. As the thought struck me, I felt the hair at the nape of my neck rise. Was it an eventuality? Yes, it was!

My worst fears were ascertained when, clandestinely, I procured a do-it-yourself pregnancy test kit and, during a visit to a friend's place, followed the instructions in the enclosed manual. I was pregnant with Sandeep's child. My reactions to the discovery were confused. I didn't know whether to feel elated with the fact that our love had finally taken a concrete form or to feel fearful of my father's reaction. However, one thing was certain. I had no more time to waste. I couldn't stay back in Surajpur for long. Every day was precious. I was beyond waiting for my father to come around. Destiny had made the decision for me.

I rushed back to Delhi, unperturbed by the cold farewell my father gave me. It was by pure design that he would only get the letter I had left for him once he returned home from the bus stand, else, knowing him, he might have opted to strangulate me with his own bare hands instead. I had not only deprived him of his right to choose a groom for his lone daughter but I had also sullied the family name by engaging in the unthinkable. He was a true-blue Rajput and, as the bus wheeled out of the Surajpur depot, I knew that I would never see my father or even set foot on that soil ever again.

Sandeep! Well, what do I say? He wasn't prepared for marriage just as yet, he reasoned, suggesting that we abort the child. Like a fool I had been expecting him to jump with joy on hearing the news. Suddenly a blanket of gloom had befallen my life and I found myself unable to see through it, incapable of thinking clearly even.

I was obviously unqualified to raise a child on my own, so I went ahead with Sandeep's plan and we got the foetus aborted at a shady clinic in west Delhi. It was a girl. In better times we had thought of naming her Myra.

Sandeep remained with me for the half-day stay at the clinic that the procedure demanded, even dropping me back to the hostel in his car later. But we didn't speak a word during the long drive. I was too weak for words and shocked too. That evening, when he left, I felt that a bolt of lightning had struck and propelled us in opposite directions. I knew that we could no more look each other in the eye now. Our relationship had surpassed its crescendo and moved into a zone of eerie silence. If Sandeep pleaded or begged even, I couldn't bring myself to forgive him. In time I realised that he had harboured no intentions of begging or pleading with me either.

From a dream-like existence, I had suddenly been sucked into a bottomless pit and I found myself groping in the dark for a support of any kind. Sandeep was no longer there, I had brutally severed my ties with my family with no hopes for redemption and my wounds were as fresh as the morning dew, only nowhere as soothing. This was when I slipped once again, so low that it is an effort to even write it here. But I have promised you not to hold back on anything… so…

Some girls from my hostel were leading dual lives, a student or a professional by the day and an escort by the night, to meet the financial demands of their lifestyles. For me it was a matter of survival. I joined them. Yes, I sold myself for money. Although I haven't managed to justify it to my own self, in my defence, though I don't expect you to understand it entirely, it didn't seem as grave a wrong then as it does now. The girls around me were all flourishing in this profession. I needed the money. Moreover, what was left for me to lose anyway? Hadn't Sandeep already snatched away everything that I might have considered preserving?

I entertained men. Avantika Rathore of Surajpur Estate would allow strange men to touch her, disrobe her, feel her body and possess her. I would make them crave for me, cringing somewhere deep within as I did so, so that they doled out a reasonable tip. Yes Rahul, as much as you might want to believe otherwise, this is indeed my ugly truth. Your Avantika has slept with strange men, countless many of them. I have lived the life of a prostitute.

Anyway, if I thought I had found a solution to my miseries by this compromise, I had another problem coming, a much more terrifying one. It all began when I was forced to visit the doctor for some gynaecological problems I had been experiencing. The problem had been there for a while but the environment I had grown up in, the absence of a mother, had prevented me from discussing it with any of the other girls. It was only when my vaginal discharges became highly frequent, threatening of causing embarrassment in public, that I could bring myself to see the doctor. I had no way of knowing how telling this deliberate delay was going to prove for me.

I was diagnosed with cervical cancer. The disease was already in an advanced stage when it was discovered (IV-B, as the doctor pointed out) with the cancer having spread to several parts of the body beyond the cervix. My bladder, intestines, lungs and liver were all infected and the only hope, if any, was to kill the cancerous cells through external radiation therapy.

Those were the loneliest days of my life. Even the doctor, while first sharing my test reports, wanted a member of my family to accompany me. I had to tell her that I had no family.'

Avantika, suffering from cervical cancer! I remembered her exuberant disposition, her zest for life, and it was amply evident why I had failed to notice the paleness her face concealed or the sadness within her eyes. My heart was beating faster as I resumed reading.

'I would remain in my bed, thinking and rethinking the terrible things I had read about the disease since it had shown up within me. I would look for someone to blame: My father, for being ignorant about a disease which is the second largest cause for cancer deaths among women across the globe and a simple vaccine that could have saved me from it; Sandeep, for propelling me towards a life that I had not envisioned in my wildest dreams and one which clearly didn't agree with me; and my own self, for being the way I had been: impressionable, naïve and stupid. But it was simply too late for reminiscences and regrets now. The damage had already done.

I was living a piteous existence, dragging myself to the hospital for one painful session upon another, drenching my pillow with my tears through the night and keeping generally to myself, cut-off and aloof from the world around. I had no one to talk to. I could talk to no one about my situation. Soon, the little money I had saved began to run out. The treatment was expensive. That was about the time I ran out of patience. I was tired of what was happening to me and wanted to put an end to it, immediately. I bought a bottle of sleeping pills and carried it to my room with me one night. My mind was made and there was no two ways about what I was going to do.

However, I allowed myself the leniency of an hour. It had been months that my mind had done anything but lament and it was only fair that I allowed it one last stroll of leisure before putting an end to its outings, forever. It was this hour of unperturbed contemplation I gave myself that turned out to be my saviour. For that little while, my thoughts didn't seem like they were my own. It was as if they were being transmitted from a source, a supreme entity, which had managed to unravel the mysterious purpose behind human existence.

Life is only as incomplete as we believe it to be, and my life, shortened as it was, wasn't yet incomplete. I thought about the numerous people I had come across going about life with handicaps much severe than mine. There were sightless people, who, never in their lives had seen the panoramic beauty of the world around them, and yet they were living. There were those, who, with their amputated limbs were forced to drag themselves from place to place in their zest for life, and yet they were living. I might have little life left ahead of me, but I was better equipped to derive the most from it than most of these people. It wasn't a curse that I knew I was going to die, it was a blessing, for it gave me the impetus to rise above trivialities and go about living each day to its fullest.

When I emerged from the bed I was a changed person. I was no longer gripped by piety and instead I found myself rearing to take on life with a renewed vigour. Only this time I was capable of calling right from wrong and good from evil. I was aware of the side I was going to align with and I wasn't going to make the same mistakes twice.

I got myself a job, shifted out of the hostel and started afresh with my life. I did everything that I had always wanted to do – travel to various parts of the world, soak in the beauty of God's creations, experiment with food I had only ever read of, sip the most exotic drinks known to mankind and try to make every passing moment a happy and memorable one. I wanted to erase the blotch I had cast on my family name. If not someone who he could be proud of, I wanted to die a daughter that my father wasn't at least ashamed of.

There was one thing however that I had pledged to stay away from – Love. My first disastrous experience with it notwithstanding, I didn't think I was left with enough time to fall in love. Moreover, it didn't make sense to engage in something that was bound to end in all-round grief. And then I met you… and Myra.

There must be a reason why they call love blind. By the time I realised what was happening, I was helplessly bound within its indissoluble clutches. I didn't know whether it was Myra, who reminded me of the daughter I could have had, or you, who, despite your resolute exterior, were a man desperately in need of tender affection and care. I was soon experiencing a burst of emotions I didn't think I was capable of. Surprisingly though, I was enjoying it more than anything else, ever.

Unable to control myself, I kept coming back until I had made a place for myself in your lives. I had found the family that had remained elusive all along. Sometimes, like my last night in Mumbai, my emotions came perilously close to breaking my self-imposed shackles and exposing themselves, but somehow I succeeded in restraining them. I was aware of your feelings for me, though I suspect you had still not come to terms with them, but my time was ebbing and I did not want our acknowledgment of love to stand in the way of the fate that I had already resigned to.

Thank you Rahul… to you and to Myra… for making my last days so wonderful that I think I can now die in peace. Your memories shall remain preserved within me till eternity and beyond. You have given me a reason to live beyond life itself and for that I shall remain eternally grateful.'

A lone tear carved its path down my eyes. I had a sinking feeling about what the next part of Avantika's letter contained. The reading was becoming an increasingly challenging task. Her face had started to appear in the words I read, smiling at me, making me feel the jab of her pain and sufferings. I picked up a glass of water from the table and as I sipped on it, I glanced at the man across the table who I was sharing this strange, turbulent moment with.

'Our families have known each other for generations… She was like a daughter to me, a sweet child…,' he mumbled nervously under my gaze before picking up a handkerchief to dab his eyes. It was only a fleeting display of emotions by the man, but enough to reveal the intensity of his anguish. In that moment I felt a strange oneness with him, the camaraderie of shared grief. But not meaning to elongate his moment of discomfort, I returned my attention to the Avantika's letter.

'By the time you get this letter, I would have departed already. Please forgive me, if you can, for not giving you the chance to say a final goodbye.'

The tears I thought I had successfully negotiated returned into play instantly. This time, rushing down my cheeks in a stream, uncontrolled and furious, but I was beyond bothering about them now.

'When I came to Mumbai last, it was right after I had paid my doctor a visit. He had summoned me to break the news that I was left with less than a month to live. As per my latest test reports, the treatment was no longer effective in containing the cancerous growth. There was nothing more that the doctor, or medical science in its extant evolved avatar, could do to elongate my life. I was going to die soon, it was certain, only the exact calendar day and time was left for God to decide.

A part of me wanted to die in your arms, holding Myra close to me as I took my last breath, but I don't think I would have had the strength to bear the sight of your pain. It would have killed me even before the appointed hour. So I chose to be selfish and abandoned you. Even now I can't help but think that I should have stayed in Mumbai for a few more days, spent some more time with Myra and you, but deep down I am aware that the longer I had opted to stay, the more excruciating my departure would have become. Moreover, my condition was fast deteriorating and I didn't want to leave you with a frail and feeble image of me. I wanted you to remember me as the same Avantika who had dropped water on you on that fateful flight.

So, I chose to return to Surajpur. I wasn't sure how my father would react to my return, but I guess the sight of your own child in pain makes people do strange things. He not only hugged me and cried like a child but has even forgiven all my past blunders. I am glad, as it provides closure to the only other loop of my life that had remained open. The first loop, I hope I am able to close by way of this letter.

You may choose to share my story with Myra or to instead tell her that I simply vanished without a trace. You could even apply your own judgment to prune the story to a form suitable for her impressionable mind. But do me a favour Rahul - please tell Myra that nothing is going to happen to her. Her life is not going to be mercilessly cut short like mine was. I will not allow that to happen, whether in my life or in my death. She is going to live with her Papa and grow up to become a daughter that he will be extremely proud of.

I have left some papers with Mr. Sethmalani. It is a trust fund that my grandfather had left for me and of which I have little use now. I have transferred it in Myra's name with you as her caretaker. The value of the fund, as Mr. Sethmalani's office informs me, should be a little over Rs 11 crore. I know you would not want to accept my money, but don't be under the impression that I am leaving this for you. This money is Myra's and you have no business poking your nose between us. Get that?

Please ensure that Myra gets the best treatment that money can buy and all else that she desires from life. Take good care of her, as I know you will, and of yourself too. Find yourself a good girl and get married. You need someone to look after you, to cuddle up to you, to tell you that you are a nice man, no matter how hard you try to make it seem otherwise.

I guess that is all I have to say. I am sure you are brimming with things you want to tell me, but we will have to stall that for another day, another life. Forgive me Rahul, if you can. Whatever I did was only because my love for you made me do it'.

As I walked down the steps of the building, Avantika's letter and the trust fund documents in my hand, it felt like my legs had turned as heavy as an elephant's. It seemed as if I was walking in a dream and nothing around me was real anymore. I wasn't even sure if I should call it a dream or a nightmare, for the cruel face of life that I had come aware of had left me shattered and trembling from within. I had reached where the rainbow ends. I had even found my pot of gold. But was I strong enough to cope with all that I had lost along the way? I didn't know.

Avantika had come into my life like a breeze of fresh air, fragrant and refreshing. She was always there whether it was my sorrows I needed to share with her or my exultations. Come to think of it, there wasn't much happiness I got to share with her, but not once did she complain. She was happy just being there, oozing affection and love, selflessly, with no desires in return. It was I who had failed to give her the due. It was I who had failed to express my gratitude, let alone my love, to her.

'The pain of regret is the worst any man can inflict upon himself,' Shalini's father's words unceremoniously rang within my ears. Was I destined to live with the burden of unproclaimed love for the rest of my life? Only if I had one chance to go back in time and bare my heart out to her. What wouldn't I give for just those ten minutes with Avantika? And yet, when she was there with me, I had remained too preoccupied with my own problems to even spare a thought for her.

There would be no such chance, I knew. Avantika was dead. She was gone and yet my heart refused to believe that she would be there no more. Somewhere I was still hoping that when I would open the doors to my house, she would be sitting there, playing with Myra.

I reached home, unlocked the doors and saw Myra. She was playing with the maid. Avantika was not there. She would not return. Never ever!

Now that I look back, Shalini had been an unripe love affair, an infatuation of sorts, just like Sandeep had been for Avantika. The only difference being that in my case the flame had held on for much longer before it abruptly extinguished. After Shalini I had lost faith in the very institution of love. I had come to believe that such a thing as true and selfless love existed only within the pages of story books.

It was Avantika who had restored my faith in the phenomenon of love. I was certain now that love existed and yet I knew that with her demise, I had been rendered incapable of loving anyone else. She had asked me to find myself a girl and get married. That was one wish I wasn't going to be able to grant her.

I looked at Myra once again. Avantika had left me with the means to end my problems, but the problems had not ended just as yet. I still had the daunting task of Myra's treatment staring me in the face. Involuntarily my fists clenched and my jaws tautened. I was bracing myself for the journey ahead. Myra was going to get all that Avantika had wished for her – the best treatment and the very best of everything that life had to offer. I was going to ensure that she got it all, if not for my own sake then for Avantika's. This was the least I could do for her and I wasn't going to shirk away from this one responsibility. Not now. Not ever.

Epilogue

Five years hence…

Without taking his hands off the steering wheel, Rahul glanced at his mobile phone screen once again. He was whizzing past the Western Express Highway in his Honda Civic car, returning after meeting a client about a deal he was expecting to close soon. The incessantly buzzing phone had been annoying him for a while now. He eyed the number before relegating the instrument to the empty passenger seat. The phone was from a landline number he didn't recognise. He didn't have the time to receive the call. He was on his way to keep an appointment he couldn't afford to be delayed for.

Myra's school was celebrating its annual day today and the children were staging a play to mark the occasion. Though Myra had only two miniscule parts in it, one playing a tree and the other, a wild animal, a deep throaty growl being her only dialogue in the entire presentation, he nevertheless had to get there in time for the event.

'I wish she had inherited her acting skills from her mother rather than me,' he thought. 'If not the protagonist, she would at least have got a more substantial role to play.'

Myra's ailment was a thing of the distant past now. Though the bone marrow transplant and watching his little girl lie on the hospital bed, pierced with countless needles, sapped and frail, had been nothing short of a nightmare for Rahul, the end proved justification enough for the means. Myra recovered eventually, regaining her vitality and youthful exuberance in little time. She was in class five now, attending her old school in Juhu and performing exceptionally well in academics. She was a keen participant in extra-curricular activities especially dramatics, but Rahul didn't see much of a career for her in acting.

Avantika's bequeathal had proved to be just the shot that Rahul's dwindling fortunes had been waiting for before taking a sharp U-turn. He was able to retain his daughter's custody but not without another fiercely fought courtroom battle. With Ramesh Sethmalani representing him, there was little doubt that the verdict could go against him.

While he still remembered the look on Shalini's face from when the Judge had delivered his verdict, his most gratifying moment in the entire episode had come at the very beginning when he had called Shalini's father to inform him that he was rejecting his offer. 'Myra is staying with me and that is final. You can go ahead and do anything you want, but you are not going to take my daughter away from me,' Rahul had said. The old man had been too stunned to respond.

A few months after Myra was discharged from the hospital, Arden had found an investor for his business, a Singapore based Private Equity firm. The firm had agreed to plough in a significant amount of capital against a 51% stake in the company, propelling the value of Rahul's 2% equity into orbit. The new owners had contracted both Arden and Rahul to run the day to day operations of the business for the next five years.

Availability of sufficient funds had enabled the duo to advertise their offerings, resulting in a substantial expansion of their customer base. It had also become much easier for them to woo suppliers, who, with the added benefit of seeing their products advertised, were no longer sceptical in doling out the required discounts. Business was good and Rahul was eyeing a renewal of his employment contract which was set to expire in five months' time. Arden meanwhile had come up with another business idea he was itching to try out. He intended to part ways with the company once his contractual obligations were over, leaving Rahul at the helm of affairs.

Shalini, Rahul had learnt through some common friends, had married a software professional about two years back. His heart went out to the guy and he hoped that Shalini had matured somewhat since they were last together, not for her but for her husband's sake. He hadn't heard about a divorce filing as yet, which was a positive sign.

The last he had spoken with Shalini was to check if she would be willing to sell their old flat back to him, at the going market price of course. She had flatly refused. The house was not an investment that she would look to profit from, it was a medium for her to torment Rahul, the only one she was left with, and she was not going to let go of it, irrespective of the price. Rahul had instead settled for another house in the same locality, marginally larger than the one he had previously owned, and shifted back to Juhu. Myra was glad to be back in her old neighbourhood and to be attending her old school once again.

Since his chance meeting with Anand, Rahul had remained in regular touch with him. The first call he made to Anand upon his return to Mumbai had been to inform him about Avantika's letter. Anand was highly sympathetic, partly curious too perhaps, and their conversation had lasted nearly an hour. It was painful, narrating Avantika's tragic tale, but in the end Rahul was glad to have found someone he could speak his heart out to.

When the court proceedings, the renewed battle for Myra's custody, had forced him to travel to Delhi once again, Rahul had put aside some time to pay Anand the visit he had promised. It was during this visit, sipping on a glass of beer in Anand's drawing room, that Rahul had impulsively asked him about Rhea and her manager, Satish.

'You knew I wouldn't let the slimeball escape, didn't you?' he had replied, smiling. 'Yes, I put my men behind Satish and he was apprehended red-handed trying to strike a deal with a decoy customer. He is comfortably lodged in Tihar Jail now, serving his sentence. Once Satish was out of the equation, there was little left for Rhea to do in Delhi. Last I heard, she had sold the flat in Chhatarpur and returned to her hometown with the proceeds. I guess that augers well for her. She at least has a hope of starting afresh now.'

Rahul had managed to reach Myra's school, successfully negotiating the crazy Mumbai traffic with twenty minutes still left before she took the stage. Parking the car in a lane outside, he headed for the school gate. He was crossing a bunch of nameless pavement stalls on the roadside when something caught his eye. It was the headline of a newspaper dangling from a hook atop a magazine stand. It had been a busy day and he had had an early start, not having the time to even flip through the newspaper. He had missed the glancing even at the headlines.

'Irrigation scam washes down Rs 750 crore. Jaidev Saxena in CBI custody,' the bold print read.

Just then his phone buzzed once again. This time though, frowning slightly at the persistence of the caller, he decided to take the call. 'Sir, I am calling from the Great Indian Bank. We are offering you a loan…,' he heard a female voice start with a well-rehearsed pitch, but he was quick to cut the conversation short. 'Sorry, I am not interested. Thank you,' he said, before disconnecting the call and surrendering the handset to his trouser pocket.

Once again he shifted his focus to the newspaper and his lips involuntarily curled into a smile. The name staring back at him from the headline, Jaidev Saxena, was Shalini's father and his onetime father-in-law.

From the Author's Desk

Like a mason who lays the bricks to a house, an author only provides the foundation for the book that eventually reaches his readers. There are many other unseen and often unheeded names that go behind putting together the final offering.

From the dreadful boss in office (if the author is pragmatic or efficient enough, as the case may be, to hold a day job alongside the pursuit of writing) who ever-so-frequently makes him resolve to focus harder on his writing as a potential backup for a rainy day, to the efficient Bai at home who ensures the continual supply of caffeine, the most crucial ingredient behind most words written these days, the list of people whose toil shapes a book is endless.

Not in the mood to embark upon the adventure (or misadventure, if you so please) of naming them all, I shall stick to only the most essential and significant ones here.

Since I don't intend to give up writing just as yet, the list of essential contributors must begin with my publishers Srishti and the many bloggers and reviewers who have expended their precious time in reading and writing about my past works.

Neeru, my wife, as her name being featured prominently among the acknowledgements is as essential to my survival as perhaps food, water and air. Abhishek, my brother, who was gracious enough to read the manuscript and share his two bits, not succumbing to the pressing temptation of investing his time in fiddling with his phone instead – Thank you.

Among others who have contributed significantly in making this book a reality are Atul Kumar, a friend and colleague, who not only unhesitatingly used reams of office stationary to print copies of the draft manuscript but also eventually thrust them into my hands with innumerable markings and suggestions (how many of those have actually been incorporated in the preceding pages remains a matter of pure academic interest) and Anirudha and Rashmi for bearing the sweltering Mumbai heat on several afternoons as I ravaged the bookstalls around Flora Fountain for my own fix of reads. Thank you guys!

If you are reading this, I am assuming you are doing so after having read the story. So, thank you for devoting your time to my work. I hope you liked what you read. And if, by some quirk of taste, you didn't quite like the book, I would urge you to keep your feedback carefully concealed. In fact, if faced with such an eventuality, you must most certainly recommend this book to all your friends and acquaintances. Seeing them spending their money and time on it might just be the pleasure, albeit sadistic, that you needed to make your day.

Anurag Anand
contact@anuraganand.in
http://www.facebook.com/anuraganandauthor